The Secret Bunker
Part 2: The Four Quadrants

PAUL TEAGUE

SCOTLAND'S
SECRET
BUNKER

Crown Buildings • Troywood • St Andrews
Fife • KY16 8QH
Tel: 01333-310301 Fax 01333-312040
email: mod@secretbunker.co.uk
web: www.secretbunker.co.uk

ISBN: 1502367734
ISBN-13: 978-1502367730

GET THE LATEST NEWS ABOUT THE
SECRET BUNKER TRILOGY!

More details at http://thesecretbunker.net/part2

ACKNOWLEDGEMENTS

This book was inspired by four amazing Cold War
bunkers which are located around the world.
However, this is a work of fiction and everybody in
the story is a creation of my imagination.

PART ONE: THE QUADRANTS

Chapter One

Armageddon

Twenty thousand kilometres above the Earth a reconnaissance satellite takes a snapshot image of the life below it. It has been doing this every five minutes for the past eighty-two hours. The first photograph that it took over two days ago showed a planet predominantly covered by water, with distinctive landmasses sporadically obscured by crisp white clouds. There is not sufficient definition in each of the images to tell the story of the millions of life forms on the surface, yet at this moment their very existence is in peril.

The satellite is identified by the marking 'GC-001'. It is the first of multiple devices launched two years ago by The Global Consortium to secretly record these events. Like sentinels, they watch patiently from the skies, impassively recording all activity as the entire planet is shrouded in darkness. Gone are the blue seas and bright, white clouds of the first images, they have now been obliterated by this dense and impenetrable presence.

Satellite GC-001 is just one of a vast matrix of international satellites recording this process. The story they will tell is, as yet, uncertain.

The darkness surrounding the Earth was supposed to be restorative, it was meant to breathe new life into this dying planet. But thousands of kilometres away, obscured by a still, black shroud, drones are launching from a secret bunker one by one, like wasps leaving a nest, intent on harm. They are unseen by the watching satellites whose lying images show a planet that looks peaceful and at rest as it slumbers beneath this dark, enveloping blanket. But a malevolent force has just unleashed the biggest threat that mankind has faced since the first life forms drew breath on the surface below.

Armageddon is described in the Bible as the last battle between good and evil before the Day of Judgement. In the next forty-eight hours this satellite will watch without emotion as humanity struggles not only for its own survival, but for the life of the planet which sustains it. By the end of today, one of those fighting on the side of good will draw a last breath and, soon afterwards, the surface of the Earth will begin to burn like it has just become Hell.

The Day of Judgement is today.

Targeted

This floor is bigger than all the rest. It must be the size of twenty football pitches, it is a vast subterrestrial hangar. There will be one of these in each of the bunkers, the underground control centres which form the four Quadrants of The Global Consortium.

The drones are like nothing he's ever seen before. They're smaller than the military versions that he watched in awe on the TV news programmes, but they look immediately more sinister and deadly. There are hundreds of them here, like bats in a cave, still and silent.

In an instant, the drones activate, one after the other. Red lights, the eyes of a devil, illuminate in the darkness. When all of the drones appear to be triggered, a bright shield of light sweeps across the full width of the far wall. It is a sight to behold and in any other circumstances it would be considered a spectacle of great visual beauty.

There is a deep rumble at the far side of the hangar and slowly, surely and deliberately its vast iron sides open up to reveal a dense blackness beyond. The drones launch into the darkness outside and as they enter that bleak nothingness they appear to have been swallowed up by some malevolent force. But it is not the darkness itself that is evil, it is the drones which make their deadly journeys within it.

Unseen by any human eye, they launch at regular intervals, each with a terrible mission. The red lights on the drones are not the eyes of a devil, though they may just as well be. Instead they indicate that the devices are armed, they have become a powerful weapon of destruction. Each one is intent on its deadly assignment – to completely annihilate the other three bunkers which lie beyond in the remaining Quadrants.

Lab Rat

The girl is restrained on a cold, metal operating table. She is no more than sixteen years of age. Unable to move even her fingers, let alone her arms, legs or head, she has been like this for over twenty-four hours now, given neither food nor water. Four small needles have been inserted at angles into the base of her spine. Once every hour for the past twenty-four hours a mechanized delivery system has injected four different liquids directly into her spinal cord.

She hasn't been told why she's here or why they have chosen her for these experiments. There are no others like her, she is all alone in this nightmare. Another hour is up. The machine whirs into life once again, and the serums are injected into her one by one. It is the final liquid which she dreads most, the one that results in agonizing spasms which last nearly the full hour until the next injection is administered.

She lets out a scream of pain which echoes down an empty corridor. The only person who's aware of what is going on here is the man who sits at his desk diligently monitoring the results of this experiment.

His office is plain and undecorated, there are no family photographs or pictures on the walls here. The only sign of who is he is and what he might be are displayed on the badge which is attached to his white lab coat. It reads 'Dr H. Pierce'.

Awoken

It was never intended that this fighting force should ever see the light of day. Specially selected more than eighteen years earlier, they'd been chosen as part of a series of initial experiments specifically for this purpose.

Tested under the most extreme conditions, each cryogenically frozen body in this room had been included on the basis of their consistent responses in a series of demanding and punishing simulations. Unknown to them, they had been frozen here since the tests ended, waiting for the time when their unique services might be required. That time was now.

The entire population of the Earth was in imminent danger from terrorist saboteurs, their evil ambition to extinguish all life on the planet and extract its rich mineral deposits for sale to the highest bidder. As the power surged through their cryogenic caskets and the blood began to flow once more through their male and female bodies, the awakening cohorts could never have guessed at the battle that lay before them. It would be a battle not only to preserve their own lives, but also to protect the lives of every remaining human being on the planet.

Chapter Two

Synchronicity

'Come with me!' she says. 'I've figured out how to stop it!'

I'm stunned for a moment, like a ghost has just appeared before me. I've now had over forty-eight hours to get used to this idea since I first thought I'd seen Nat just beyond the bunker doors. The possibility that she might be alive has been churning around in my head all of that time, one minute accepting the possibility, the next cruelly denying myself of any hope. Yet here she is, three years older, much taller now – the same as me – but very definitely Nat. I know it's Nat. The connection that I lost when her life was apparently extinguished right in front of me is back.

I feel the blood surging through my veins, the spark of a new energy invigorates my entire body and I am once again fully alive. This is how I'm supposed to be. It is like a fusion as we stand together here, we create an energy and it is stronger than it was before, because we are now older. Nat feels it too, she is taken aback by its velocity.

In Dad's video he said, 'It's about you, it's all about you and Nat.'

'Work together,' he'd urged, and now I understand.

Both Nat and I feel it in this instant, this synchronicity tells us everything we need to know. Neither of us can explain it yet, but we know as we stand here facing each other, nourished and energized by this incredible reunion, that the solution must reside with us. We are different from other people and we are twins.

Whatever must be done to fight the evil that has been unleashed in this place, we will face it and fight it together.

Others

The three screens in the Operations Centre on Level 3 continued to transmit their urgent messages, unheard by anybody else in the bunker. Like echoes in an empty cave, their pleas were broadcast into nothingness.

'Quadrant 2 to Quadrant 1, breaking communication protocols to transmit this urgent message,' came the repeated words.

The Operations Centre lay still and empty, there was nobody here to receive these messages. Moments beforehand a teenager had been here, one who was capable of accessing this area and responding to these people, but the doors had just closed behind him as the screens crackled into life. For now, their cries would go unheard as they became ever more desperate.

20:23 Quadrant 3: White Sulphur Springs, West Virginia

Magnus watched the screen on his console, deciding not to share it with the entire Control Room just yet. He would need time to assimilate this information, to decide how to process it himself first of all. In training simulations these events had not even been presented as a possibility. Only the bunker's Custodian was briefed on Tier 6 to Tier 10 alert scenarios, yet he had believed them to be alone in their guardianship of the planet.

He was currently tracking three drones which had just launched automatically from a location in Southern Scotland, UK. The only likely source that he could find was an old Cold War tourist attraction concealed many metres beneath a deceptive and inoffensive looking cottage. This was a pinprick compared to the much larger installation at White Sulphur Springs; it seemed hardly conceivable that a threat could have come from such an unlikely location.

By 20:00 there was to have been zero airspace activity – yet here was the evidence on screen. A fourth light appeared out of nowhere, to accompany the other three. Whatever was happening here, these drones were appearing at one-minute intervals and they were not authorized as part of the core mission outline.

Magnus consulted the E-Pad which was tied in specifically to his biometric ID code. To access guidance for Tier 6–Tier 10 alerts he'd have to triple authenticate his ID. That meant a retina scan, a sweep of brain-wave patterns and a pin-prick sample of his blood.

He moved into one of the meeting rooms that were located around the edges of the Control Room, he didn't want to draw attention to what was going on here. As Magnus entered the darkened room, in the moments before the lights detected his presence, the trained eye would have spotted a faint yellow light, just below the surface of the skin on his neck. As yet it was at rest, there was no activity, but there was very definitely some device implanted just below the surface of his skin, as if waiting for somebody far away to activate it.

Alive

He watched the pool of blood grow steadily wider as the security team congratulated him on his successful apprehension of the intruder, impervious to the fading life before them. His strategy had paid off well, nobody had registered him as being out of place here and with his limited security access to the bunker, he expected to remain undetected for some time. But to gain this freedom, he had had to take a massive chance with her life and as he watched her bleeding out in front of him, he knew that he had very little time to save her.

'I'll dispose of the body,' he volunteered. 'Kate wants her out of the way.'

The members of the security team were happy to accept this – after all, they had no reason to suspect anything now. Two of the team offered to collect a HoverTrolley from the MedLab, on which to transport the body to the cremation area.

Left alone for a few moments, he darted towards

the woman's body and took out a device from his pocket. This was not a gadget that you'd see in any normal medical facility. He held it above the area into which he had shot only minutes earlier, but now it healed rather than harmed, sealing the wound and beginning the process of tissue repair that would be required for her recovery.

The woman gave a gasp of life and looked at him directly in the eyes as if seeking an explanation for why this man should want her dead one minute and alive the next.

'Lie still,' he commanded urgently. 'I'll get you out of here, you'll need to bear the pain for a while.'

She did a good job, and he alone detected her silent wince as the security guards rolled her body contemptuously onto the HoverTrolley.

'I'll take care of it from here,' he confirmed and headed along the corridor in the opposite direction to the security team, her body still and lifeless as he'd instructed.

'Stay still,' he whispered, 'I need to get you away from the cameras.'

'You need to get to my family,' she spoke as loudly as she dared. 'They've switched off their life support.'

'I'm on it,' he replied impatiently. 'They still have a short time before they reach a critical stage. I need to take care of that bleeding first.'

He guided the HoverTrolley towards the dormitory area where only a short time earlier she'd taken sanctuary for the first time. Her bag and laptop were still by the bunks where she'd abandoned them earlier. In spite of the pain that she was in, she still scolded herself for being so careless as to leave them in plain sight.

'I'm here to help you,' he said. 'Your daughter is alive, I believe that you and your family are caught up with whatever is going on here.'

He decided that now was not the time to tell her that it was he who had killed her daughter three years earlier. She had not recognized him so far from their trip to the hospital six days ago, so he was grateful that the Neuronic Device in her neck was still doing its job by controlling the messages sent between spine and brain. He checked that it was still there – as if anything could have removed it. He saw the faint blue light beneath her skin and wondered why she'd been implanted with a blue device rather than any of the other options that were available. This was not his security level, but interesting nevertheless.

'You knew exactly where to shoot,' she said to him almost accusingly. 'How did you know that?'

'I needed to get you out of there in one piece,' he replied, 'and make it convincing.'

'You need to thank your titanium rib implants for getting you out of that one alive!'

Captive

The device in the guard's neck had been still for some time, but as James was escorted to the interrogation room, it began to glow once again. He had been exposed as an imposter and sabotaging force, and would be interrogated and punished. There was no law here now, no government to ensure his human rights.

The bunker was under the control of a new force, and they had little concern about rights and procedures. The security team which would administer this treatment was made up of good people, but they were being controlled by nanotechnology which was implanted in their necks. From there the devices made rapid neural connections between brain and spine.

The faint, pulsating glow in their necks was the only indication that these neural pathways were being manipulated by an external force.

Memories could be suppressed or enhanced, instructions given that would be executed without question or hesitation, emotions controlled and inhibited. But in the treatment of this man – James – it was their conscience that would need to be suppressed for what they were about to do next.

Chapter Three

Momentum

What do you say to the twin sister who you'd thought to be dead for the past three years when she reappears before your eyes, almost in a puff of smoke? I've seen so much since those bunker doors closed and left me alone and separated from my family in that dark corridor, that I suspect there isn't much that would surprise me now. I had been convinced at first that I was going to see my mum and family perish in front of me. That possibility has been forced upon me, retracted, and then thrust at me once again in the last forty-eight hours.

I have had to wrestle too with the possibility of my own death; it feels like I've faced more in the past few days than I have since we lost Nat. I just hug her and say her name, 'Nat', trying to erase three years of sorrow, loss and emptiness. She hugs me back, she feels it too, but we know that we have limited time here. There is no opportunity yet for catching up and exchanging stories, we have things that must be done – and fast.

'It's great to see you Nat, but how are you even here?' I say.

'I was never dead Dan,' she replies. 'It was all a set-up to make it look real.'

I knew I'd seen her move that day the accident happened, I felt in my bones that something wasn't right, but why didn't I say? I curse myself for my inaction, but who would have listened to me? I was thirteen years old at the time, I'm not even totally sure that anybody would listen now.

'We're caught up in something really big here Dan,' Nat continued. 'I've got so much I need to tell you, but we must take quick action.'

'We have to use the transportation systems together,' she says. 'I finally figured it out when you saw me earlier.

'And those weird buttons in the lift – if we press them together, they take us somewhere, I'm just not sure where yet!'

Of course, that's why the lift jolted when I touched the buttons – I was halfway there, but whatever it is that lets me operate most things here, it looks like both of us will be needed to fully activate that.

'What's all this got to do with us?' I ask Nat. 'I just don't get why we're so important!'

'There's a lot I need to tell you Dan,' says Nat, and I get the feeling that now is not the time to get into this conversation, however much I'm desperate to know.

'There's something about drones that we need to know,' I splutter. 'Some kind of terrorist has got involved with whatever is going on here and they're going to target the drones.'

'I'm slightly ahead with some of the technology here Dan,' Nat replies. 'Where I've been held, they use a lot of this stuff and I've seen how some of it works.'

This hangs in the air. Nat doesn't want to tell me something, and I decide not to probe just yet. What does she mean by being 'held'? That sounds like prison or something. And it certainly doesn't suggest that she was a volunteer there.

'We need to find Mum and James first,' I suggest. 'If we can get to them, we can make a plan.'

'I have another idea,' replies Nat.

'We need to see where that lift will take us and get out of here if we can.'

'Whatever this transporter thing does, when I disappeared just now I was in a different place.'

'It was like this area, but different. I'm sure it was in another bunker.'

I'm as keen as Nat to try the Transporter, but I need to tell her about the secret video message first.

'But Doctor Pierce said to trust Mum and James ...' I begin.

'Doctor Pierce!' she explodes. 'That man is the Devil.'

Alliance

'How did you know about the ribs though?' she asked, as he ran the electronic device once again over the wounded area. The instrument that he was using had had an immediate and massive effect on the bleeding. She felt shocked, sore and unsteady, but it had actually healed her in front of her own eyes, as if it had accelerated a biological process that would normally take months of rehabilitation like the last time she'd been shot.

'I know a lot about you and your family,' he replied, sensing that the time for secrecy was probably over.

He was too far in now, he'd committed to helping this woman and trying to find out how her child was involved. He needed to discover why he'd been in the car that had seemingly killed her.

'I work for an organization called The Global Consortium,' he began.

She was too tired now to ask questions, she just needed to rest a while and orientate herself. Mindful of whatever was happening to her family as they spoke, but deciding to trust this man for now, she indicated with a nod that he should continue speaking.

'As you heard from the announcement, we are in the middle of a terraforming process,' he continued. 'This has been planned for many years now, it's the culmination of a very long-term international initiative.

'The terraforming itself is benign and, from my restricted knowledge of the project, this is all pretty critical, but it's scheduled to take place around us.

'In simple terms, the aim is for the Earth to be healed while everybody sleeps.'

She looked at him, hanging on to every drop of information that he was imparting, struggling to come to terms with the sheer scale of what was going on.

'There's something not right though,' the man carried on, sensing how much she craved this information.

'When I saw that you were involved in this, I knew there had to be a connection with the death of your daughter ...' he started.

'Nat ...' she said, and her name just hung there for a moment.

'She's alive,' he picked up from the silence, 'but like you I was there when she died three years ago.'

'What do you know?' she began, but decided against it.

He saw that she'd thought better of it for now, and carried on with his explanation.

'You're all connected to this in some way Amy,' he said, using her name for the first time. If they were to form an alliance, that seemed more appropriate. 'You, your two eldest children and that man who came to rescue you from outside the blast doors, he must be involved in this too.

'I just can't see what it is yet, but whatever is going on, it's not how this was planned. This is a massive planet-wide operation, but for The Global Consortium it's not considered to be a massive security risk in any way. In some ways, it's the safest we could ever be: the entire world is involved in these events, they all want it to happen, they're actually all united on this.'

She could sense that there was more to come, that he was choosing his words with care.

'There's a problem with the Neuronic Devices. They seem to have been hacked in some way, the way those people in the Control Room have started behaving is not right.'

He paused, as if steeling himself.

'And Kate, the lady who's in charge of this facility,' he began, 'she hasn't recognized me yet, but I know her, and she's a good woman. She and I served in the Army together eighteen years ago, we were part of a team until we got separated after an exercise we were taking part in.

'Last thing I knew, she had been shot dead.'

20:43 Quadrant 3: White Sulphur Springs, West Virginia

Magnus worked through the data on the screen. Every way he processed this scenario, it took him to the same conclusion. But it seemed incredible, it was simply an option that hadn't been offered in training.

Magnus had believed – as had all the other four Custodians – that they were the only ones. They were charged with watching over the world from their bunker in West Virginia. The sirens had sounded at 10:00 local time and, as with the UK, all the bunker staff had gathered at the site already.

At White Sulphur Springs, the exchange of staff had been a much more managed affair, with Global Consortium personnel replacing military staff at a pre-appointed time. But Magnus, like Kate and the other Custodians, believed that they were alone, that there were no others. Magnus thought that as the major superpower in the world, the United States was alone charged with the role of caretaker of the planet.

And now, consulting his E-Pad, he was confronted with the astonishing truth. There were three more bunkers, each one controlled by one of the world's superpowers. Precise locations were not given, but there were bunkers in the UK, USA, China, and Russian Federation.

He figured that must have taken one of the biggest political charm offensives in the history of the planet. If the impending global catastrophe had not been so unavoidable, perhaps minds would not have been so focused. But the alarming reality of a planet with no more than ten years of life left tends to blow away petty political objections and make consensus more likely. Magnus was too stunned to act for a moment, but then his leadership obligations intervened.

Directives stated that only in the event of a Tier 10 alert would Custodians become aware of the other bunker facilities. This was such a crisis. His data indicated that the first drones released from their UK location were armed and targeted directly at his installation in White Sulphur Springs, West Virginia. They would take a few hours to arrive at their final, deadly destination but there was only one course of action permissible: to make immediate contact with the other three bunkers.

The pre-planning had not allowed for such a terrible scenario, this was supposed to be a routine and non-contentious operation. All countries globally were signed up to this, there was not meant to be any conflict here. So why in the last five minutes that he'd been reading his briefing notes had another cluster of drones been launched from the UK, each one armed and destined for West Virginia?

Detection

Kate continued to monitor the screens in front of her,

the red device in her neck flashing as her neural pathways were controlled by a force unknown to her and far away. The drones were launching at the rate of one per minute, every one of them programmed to seek and destroy their chosen target. The first wave was heading directly for White Sulphur Springs, the seemingly impregnable facility so many miles away in West Virginia.

Had Kate not been under the cerebral and physical control of the device buried inside her, she would have abhorred her actions and been repulsed by the events that she had set in motion. Only an hour beforehand she had been as ignorant as the other Custodians that there were any other similar facilities on the planet. Now it was her primary mission to destroy them, using drones which had been intended for post-terraforming reconnaissance.

They were there primarily to protect the Earth, not to assist in its destruction.

All around her, bunker staff went about the jobs prescribed to them via their own Neuronic implants, equally oblivious to the harm they were about to do. They had become involved in the Genesis 2 project because they passionately believed in the greater good. They were in this place, at this time, to protect the planet for future generations.

It would be challenging, difficult and complex, but at the end of the project they would be able to emerge from the bunker knowing that they had played their part in Man's greatest ever adventure. Nobody would remember these events, because only the leaders of The Global Consortium would retain knowledge of what had gone on. They were currently asleep, along with the rest of the planet, watched over by teams of specially selected personnel, chosen on the basis of careful psychometric tests over the course of several years.

Each member country of The Global Consortium would receive full data recordings from the complex matrix of satellites currently in orbit above the Earth, but no other individuals would be party to the whole story about what went on here. That information would be concealed in the annals of the world's history. Depending on the actions that Kate was about to take, it was possible that no member of The Global Consortium might ever get the chance to view the visual footage showing what happened in Earth's final hours.

Screams

The corridors in the bunker were silent places. Much of the activity centred around the Control Room on Level 2. The majority of the staff were to be found in the canteen area, in the MedLab, and in the security zones, and now that the full briefing had been delivered by Doctor Pierce, a shift pattern was coming into play, as some personnel got ready to retire for the night.

This was to be a 24/7 operation for the next fourteen days. There was not a huge staff required, but it still numbered 300 in total. The bunker was a quiet place too, so if there was a sound, an alarm or an announcement, it was very dominant and not easily missed.

It was a good job then that the interrogation room used by the security staff was located at the back of a group of rooms used by that team. If they had been slightly closer to the main corridor, staff finishing their shifts might have been alarmed to hear the agonized cries emanating from those rooms as the bunker's first captive was interrogated aggressively by the security team.

Chapter Four

Falling Out

The two young children had been left on their own for a very short time in the living room. They were barely walking – more a combination of rolling, pulling and toddling.

Surrounded by toys, it was a peaceful and harmonious scene when their parents had moved into the kitchen momentarily to make a hot drink and continue their conversation. They wouldn't be able to do this for much longer, as once the kids were fully mobile, they'd need eyes in the back of their heads.

All of a sudden, without warning or any kind of build up or provocation, one of the children grabbed a wooden block and dashed it against the head of the other child, who sat there for an instant, stunned and completely taken by surprise. Why would your sibling, who'd been playing quite happily with you only seconds ago, erupt into a spontaneous outburst of unprovoked aggression?

The dazed silence didn't last long, and the wounded child soon let out a roar of pain that had both parents back in the room in no time at all.

They were greeted by a wailing child, blood streaming quite fast from a head wound, and a second child looking innocent and unconcerned, just to the side.

Both parents were astonished for a while, in that 'how long did we leave them?' way that only adults seem to appreciate.

Both noticed something which really unsettled them later on that day, once they had returned from the hospital where the wounded child needed three stitches. They didn't talk about it, because parents fear these things in their own children, they're not aspects of a child's personality which they will readily acknowledge or admit.

The child who had inflicted the violent act had actually been smirking when they came in the room, as if that unprovoked and hostile action were actually an achievement or breakthrough. It was as if the child had just discovered violence and found it to be very much to their liking.

The Second Bunker

I'm not sure how to respond to Nat's comment about Doctor Pierce.

'The Devil' is not really a term used by people who are indifferent in their opinion, and it leaves us with a bit of a dilemma, bearing in mind that one of the people who I really do trust – Dad – told me that I should listen to him. Dad didn't seem to be under duress in that video he'd sent me. I know Doctor Pierce already from the visits at school and he certainly doesn't strike me as being anything like the Devil.

He's odd, certainly, but there is nothing demonic about him. However, things certainly aren't what they seem. After all, why would the guy who was my school psychologist be mixed up in something like this? It's a bit like finding out that your primary school teacher has a secret life as a ninja – in real life things like that just don't happen.

'What's the problem with Doctor Pierce?' I ask. 'He's a bit weird, but he seems harmless enough.'

Nat draws a deep breath, and I become aware that she is much more mature than I am now, she seems more assured, as if she has seen more of the world than me in the time that we have been apart. There is a weariness to her voice, a pain, like she's holding something back. I sense that she has a lot to tell me, that it could all come flooding out at once, but that she doesn't know where to start and we just don't have the time.

'There's a lot I need to tell you Dan,' she begins, but she doesn't get a chance to finish.

A voice booms out from the announcement system, making us both jump. We thought we were alone down here, so we weren't expecting anybody else's voice. It is Doctor Pierce again.

'Quadrants 2, 3 and 4 please assemble for an unscheduled briefing in five minutes,' he announces. 'Attendance of all staff is compulsory.'

The speaker, wherever it is, goes quiet. I look at Nat, she looks at me. The unspoken question just hangs there. Do we trust Doctor Pierce or not? And what's all this about Quadrants 2, 3 and 4?

'Look Nat,' I say, 'whatever you think about Doctor Pierce, he's our best bet for getting around here. He appears to be in charge of this place, and he certainly seems to think that I'm okay to speak to.

'How about we listen to what he has to say, don't play awkward, and figure out this thing for ourselves as we go along?'

Nat considers this, and then drops a bit of a bombshell.

'Nobody knows I'm here yet,' she begins. 'I ...'

She pauses. This is difficult for her, I hate to think what's been going on since we last saw each other.

'I escaped from them,' she finally continues. 'They're hunting for me.'

'Who's hunting for you?' I ask. I really feel like somebody dropped me into the middle of an action movie here and I'm just catching up with the plot.

'Doctor Pierce and the others,' she carries on. 'They'll be very interested to know that I'm here.'

It's me who decides to show maturity and good judgement at this point, and not for the first time since all this started kicking off, I see things with clarity.

'Nat, let's go to the Operations Centre and get this message. You need to stay away from the screens. Let's make out like I'm on my own still and hear what Pierce has to say. That way we stay in control of this situation, the worst thing that can happen to us is to be separated now. We also need to find Mum before we use these Transporters – if we can group together, we can agree a way ahead in all of this.'

Nat looks at me and smiles.

'We've both done some growing up since we last saw each other Dan,' she says. 'It's great to be back.'

I feel the same, it's just amazing to have her back, however it happened and whatever is going on here, it's just so good to be together again. There will be time to sort all of this out, to catch up and hear Nat's story, but for now we both know that we have to focus on the pressing issues like finding Mum, Dad,

Harriet and David – and we need to figure out what's going on with Doctor Pierce. These drones, whatever they are, need sorting out too; I have a feeling that if we can hook up as a family again, together with that guy that Mum seems to know, we can figure this out between us. What a family reunion that's going to be.

Nat and I head for the Operations Centre on Level 3. As we press the button in the lift, I can tell that she's as tempted as I am to put those strangely marked buttons to the test, but now is not the time. This must mean I'm becoming more like an adult, however young and daft I still feel at times. There was a time when we'd have pressed those buttons, just for the thrill, like we'd just zoomed off on a brand new fairground ride, not sure if we were going to enjoy it or be terrified, but too young to appreciate the consequences. Now we know that other people are relying on us, it's not just about us at the moment. I still can't wait to press those buttons though.

We make our way to the Operations Centre. I'm not sure if Nat has been here yet, she looks around as we walk, taking it all in. She doesn't seem surprised by it, and that seems unusual to me. It's as if she's seen things like this before.

When we walk into the Operations Centre, my heart suddenly jumps because I think that we've walked into an area where there are other people. I'm mistaken, although there are voices coming from the screens. In fact there are three faces there: two men, one woman, and they're all speaking at once. They don't appear to know who they're talking to, neither do they appear to know that they're all speaking at once. Who are these people?

I wouldn't claim to have seen everybody in this

bunker yet, but they are all dressed in different uniforms and they are all clearly broadcasting from areas not dissimilar to the Control Room on the upper floor. But it is definitely not the same Control Room that Kate is in.

Their messages are on a video loop I think. They're not live broadcasts as far as I can tell, but they are certainly distress calls. They're referring to the drones and obviously in a panic because they are under threat of attack. That ties in with what Doctor Pierce told me.

'I know you hate him,' I say to Nat who has been taking in the video messages alongside me, 'but I think we have to play along with Doctor Pierce to find out what's going on.'

As if on cue, the main screen on the Operations Centre lights up and Doctor Pierce's face fills it entirely. He looks tired and anxious, he is unsettled and nervous.

'Maybe you should hide?' I suggest to Nat, 'in case it's a two-way screen?'

'It's fine,' she replies, 'I've seen these things before. The two-way camera above the screen is inactive at the moment, a little light comes on when they can see us. This is a one-way message, an announcement, so we're fine for now.'

Doctor Pierce begins to speak. The three smaller screens continue to broadcast their looped messages; it's very distracting, but Doctor Pierce seems to have got the edge on volume. As he begins to make his announcement on the main screen, the console to my side, where my phone had magically recharged, suddenly surges into life.

It looks like I'm about to get another private

message from Doctor Pierce.

21:07 Quadrant 3: White Sulphur Springs, West Virginia

Magnus and his team gathered in the Control Room for the unscheduled announcement from Doctor Pierce. Hopefully this would give some clarity about the drones, as they wouldn't take long before they reached their destination and began to release their missiles on the bunker.

Although it was built securely underground, it had been created primarily to withstand general atomic bomb blasts, not a constant and targeted assault from the air. As Doctor Pierce began his message, it was immediately clear to Magnus that he was uncomfortable. He looked, for want of a better word, to be rattled.

'This is a secured message for Quadrants 2, 3 and 4 only,' he began.

That's four bunkers in all. Magnus had thought – they'd all thought – that there was only one bunker monitoring these events. Their bunker.

'I am sure that you will be surprised to hear that you are not alone in your mission,' the Doctor continued, as if he'd read Magnus's mind.

'It is true, there are four bunkers positioned in locations around the world, each one known as a Quadrant. Together, you form the core teams in the Genesis 2 project.

'You are all charged with a different, unique and crucial mission during the terraforming process, and you were to have remained unaware of the teams working in the other Quadrants.

'That I am sharing this information with you now is an indication of the gravity of the situation which we now face together.

'This was to have been an entirely peaceful process, with the full agreement and cooperation of all members of The Global Consortium.'

He paused, and looked tired and weary.

'It seems that the operation has been sabotaged, though at this moment I cannot tell you by whom. However, as you will have seen on your screens, drones have been launched from Quadrant 1 in Scotland and these are heavily armed and heading for each one of your own Quadrants.

'Genesis 2 teams, you are all in very real peril, and the future of our planet lies in our hands right now. It seems that all personnel in Quadrant 1 are working with these saboteurs – these terrorists – and consequently threatening the regeneration of our planet.'

He said the word 'terrorists' with contempt, as if this was personal.

'It is unclear why they are doing this and what their purpose is,' he continued, 'but we are all at very great threat here, and that includes your own loved ones on the surface of the planet who rely on you totally as their guardians right now.'

Magnus gulped at that. He knew that this was a role with great responsibility, and he was certainly up to the job, but this was not quite how he'd anticipated things playing out.

'Ladies and gentlemen, guardians of the Genesis 2 project, I believe Quadrants 2, 3 and 4 to be free of terrorist infiltration at this moment in time, but how long that situation will remain, I cannot be sure.

'We need to be vigilant at all times, we are now on full alert status.'

Magnus noted the uneasiness around him in the room. He would need to show leadership and authority once this announcement had ended, this was no longer just an administrative role for him.

'There is one person who can navigate us through this treachery, and you must welcome him in your bunker if he makes himself known to you.

'I cannot reveal why for security reasons, but this boy has a very special role to play in this scenario and he is the only one who can help us today. His name is Dan Tracy, and here is a photograph of him.'

A photo of a young adult appeared on the screen; Magnus looked at it particularly closely, though it should be easy to spot a child in this place, everybody else around him was a highly trained adult.

'I cannot reveal my own whereabouts at the present time as it is crucial that I am able to act as a conduit of communication during this crisis. However, I am at a secure location and in direct contact with your three Quadrants.

'At this time, nobody who is presently conscious on this planet knows where I am, and it needs to stay that way for now. This is how The Global Consortium planned this process before the terraforming began.

'I will continue to update you as I am able to glean more information about this terrorist attack. In the meantime, please remain vigilant and give Dan Tracy anything he needs if he contacts you. He's a bright lad, I have every faith that he will figure this out.'

Magnus was ready to turn away, thinking this was the end of the announcement, but Doctor Pierce drew breath once again, deciding at the last minute to add a little more.

'Quadrants 2, 3 and 4, our focus now is to disable the drones, this can only be done with the help of Dan Tracy. He will make contact with one of your Quadrants soon, be ready when he comes.'

Chapter Five

21:17 Quadrant 2: Balaklava Bay, Crimea

Viktor sighed to himself, taking great care not to show what he was thinking. Like the other Custodians of the remaining Quadrants, he'd also now accessed the Tier 10 documentation which he was never supposed to see as part of this mission. He too had been alerted to the drones from Southern Scotland heading off on the radar to three unknown destinations around the world. Doctor Pierce had at least clarified that point – they were not alone in this as he had thought … as they had all thought. And it was now very clear exactly where those drones were heading.

Viktor thought of his wife and two daughters at home, in a sleep of oblivion like the rest of the world's population. This was no time for sentimentality. As a man with a military background, he knew that their security, survival and well-being now depended on people just like him. He would do what he had to do to work with the other Quadrants and defend the planet against this latest threat.

This had been part of the training and testing that had culminated in his taking this position in the first place, the ability to make the correct decisions in moments of extreme stress when all of the information around you is changing from minute-to-minute. Yes, Viktor knew what had to be done. He'd seen war and conflict before and he knew when it was the time to fight for your life.

Saved

She was not so much taken aback by the fact that he'd seen Kate shot dead – or so he'd thought. She'd already been on the receiving end of too much shooting herself, she'd be happy to never have to see a gun ever again. And that included on the TV.

More surprising to her was that he seemed to be describing a mirror incident to what she'd experienced with James.

'What happened with you and Kate?' she asked, sensing that this was all linked.

'I don't have time to go into detail right now,' he said, 'but let's just say the last time we were in the same room together it was as part of a military exercise. Only we messed up their plan and shot each other,' he continued. 'We didn't kill each other – as you can see!' he added, realizing how obvious that was as he said it.

'Funnily enough, this device I'm holding now came out of that same exercise. It's an amazing thing, it massively accelerates the healing process in non-fatal injuries. It just takes what Mother Nature does slowly and speeds it up many hundreds of times. It's why I took the gamble to shoot you. Sorry about that.'

She was beginning to understand why he'd had to do what he'd just done. After all, she'd made similar decisions in her own life. Poor old James.

Not only had she shot him, she'd now whacked him on the head. So she understood the necessity of hard decisions like these in times of stress. This man seemed to have been through a similar experience to James and herself. Why then were they all gathered in this place together? It had to be connected with those Army exercises all those years ago.

And then there was Nat of course. Nat was back, how could that possibly be? Before her mind began to wander off, she snapped back into decision-making mode.

Her wound was sore and uncomfortable, but – miraculously – healed. It had actually healed right in front of her eyes. Incredible.

She was quite clear about what needed to be done next. Kate and her team thought she was dead. She needed to change her appearance and stick close to this man. He was a security 'hero' so, as long as she looked different and stayed with him, nobody should be looking at her too closely.

Next priority was the safety of her family. Mike, David and Harriet were in imminent danger, they had to be rescued first. Then Dan … and Nat. She needed to find them as soon as possible. And James was crucial in all of this too.

The bunker wasn't that big – surely it couldn't be too hard to locate everybody? It wasn't as if they could go anywhere. She held out her hand. 'I'm Amy, thanks for shooting me,' she said drily.

'Simon!' he replied, taking her hand and shaking it.

'I don't know what's going here Amy,' he continued, 'but I want to help you and your family get out of this and figure out with you how all of this is connected.'

'I'm with you on that,' she replied. 'We need to find a disguise for me first, then we must sort out Mike and the kids.'

'I'm ahead of you,' said Simon, and he indicated some lockers to her right, where an array of different uniforms were hung.

Around the dormitory area were various bits and pieces that staff had left by bedsides and in drawers. They hadn't brought a lot – there were no suitcases or anything like that – just a few bits that could be carried in small bags so that they looked like regular tourists when they arrived here.

It wasn't long until she'd changed her appearance. A hair tie here, a pair of glasses there, a different coloured uniform and a clipboard in hand and she was transformed. Well, enough at least not to be spotted, bearing in mind she was supposed to be dead.

The new allies headed along the corridor towards the BioFiltration Area. This was where Kate had imposed a sentence of death on her family. It wasn't Kate who'd done this of course, but whoever was controlling her via the Neuronic Device in her neck. She was simply a host body for some malevolent entity, completely oblivious to the terrible actions which she had set in motion.

Amy and Simon entered the BioFiltration Area, and it was very clear that they had little time left. You didn't have to be a medical professional to see that the life support data on the screens to the side of each cocooned body was not looking good.

It was the bright red alert graphics which probably gave it away. Simon made directly for a panel in the corner of the room and pulled it away. It revealed a complex system of cables, lights and electronics. He studied it for a while, then grabbed a cluster of cables and ripped them all out at once. There were electrical sparks for a few seconds then silence.

All of the BioFiltration units closed down, the life support panels dying instantly.

'What have you done?' shouted Amy urgently, as the lights in her family's caskets faded to black.

Secret Broadcast

Doctor Pierce begins to speak.

'This is a secured message for Quadrants 2, 3 and 4 only ...' he starts.

There's too much going on all of a sudden. It's like walking into a TV shop with loads of different channels broadcasting all at once.

I can't focus.

'Nat, you listen to that one!' I say, in a voice that's much more assertive than I'd normally use.

That's just what Nat wants, to return from goodness knows where after three years just to have her twin brother pushing her around.

She realizes why I'm saying it though, and nods in agreement.

There is a small ear device at this console and I pop it into my right ear. At least I hope that's what it's for. My hunch turns out to be correct, because for the second time today I am receiving a dedicated message from Doctor Pierce or 'the Devil' as Nat prefers to refer to him.

'Dan, this is an encrypted message, I'm not sure how much longer I'm going to be able to send these undetected.

'I can tell from monitoring your Quadrant that you've found your way around already – I always knew you were a smart lad.'

I wasn't expecting flattery to be part of this, but now you mention it …

'Dan, I don't have time to explain everything to you now, it's very complicated and there's so much for you to take in. Please trust me though, and trust your dad's judgement in passing that video message on to you.'

He paused.

'You're going to need to make a lot of fast decisions about who to trust in the next couple of hours. Please be assured that I am one of those people.'

I think back to what Nat called him again. Is this man the Devil? Is he manipulating me here?

Doctor Pierce carries on. I don't think this is a two-way conversation as he isn't asking me any questions and besides I can't see a microphone anywhere.

'You need to stop the drones first Dan – you can do that by communicating with one of the other Quadrants. You're in the right place to do that right now. I suggest you speak to Magnus first, he's in the Energy Quadrant.

'There's a lot to take in here Dan, but there are four bunkers – Quadrants as we call them. You are Quadrant 1, Quadrant 2 is in Crimea, Quadrant 3 in West Virginia, and Quadrant 4 in Beijing. Each bunker has a different primary purpose. Your bunker is technology.

'Quadrant 2 is hydroponics and biology, 3 is the

energy hub, and Quadrant 4 is science. They're built for interdependency; in the eventuality of a crisis, all the bunkers must depend on each other for survival.'

He frowns.

'We built them that way Dan, but it was never supposed to come to this. I still can't believe that we've been sabotaged.

'Each bunker was supposed to monitor the terraforming in isolation, they were not supposed to know about each other's existence.

'We class this sabotage of the drones as a Tier 10 event – that means that I've had to divulge some of this information to the Genesis 2 Custodians.

'Quadrants 2, 3 and 4 seem unaffected by the terrorists as far as I can tell, but I don't know how long it will stay that way. Once they take over Quadrant 1 they can start to exert their control over the tech.

'Dan, there is something unique about you and your sister – well you at least – that makes you key to all this.'

He doesn't seem to know about Nat yet. That's a good thing for now, but puzzling. But why did he mention Nat as if she's no longer with us?

'You can stop the drones Dan. Hook up with Magnus in Quadrant 3, together you'll be able to disable them.

'I have to go, my main broadcast is ending now, I'll send an encrypted update whenever I make a general announcement, but eventually they'll detect them and block them.

'A couple more things Dan, quickly …'

I can tell he's pressed for time now, he looks like he's beginning to wind up his announcement on the main screen. One of these must be recorded I'm guessing.

'Grab some Comms-Tabs from the Weaponry Room, that way you can securely speak to your mum and James when you find them. They'll stay secure until Kate and her team discover the lower levels – when they figure out there are more levels to the bunker, the Comms-Tabs may no longer be secure.

'You've got about an hour to disable the drones, and then they'll start to reach their targets. The bunkers will be able to withstand a few hours of concentrated firing, then they'll begin to fall.

'Finally Dan, do you have anything of your sister with you – a memento like a lock of hair for instance? If we can access her DNA, you can get into all four Quadrants, you're the only one who can do that Dan. It's because of what – who – you are …'

He finishes mid-sentence, his main announcement has ended, and that triggers the abrupt termination of his encrypted message too.

21:52 Quadrant 4: Dixia Cheng, Beijing

Xiang looked nervously at the dots on her screen. They appeared so harmless at the moment, but she knew that each of those dots represented a heavily armed drone. Currently they were clustered over Denmark; they'd strike all of the bunkers within two to three hours of each other. There must have been over forty drones heading towards the USA, many more towards Europe. She knew that shortly the larger cluster would separate off, and one group would head for Crimea, while the other would be targeted at her own base in Beijing. Such massive firepower: heavily armed and destined for just three locations.

She'd had some time to think through what Doctor Pierce had said in his announcement, after giving her own personnel a briefing about security, extended shift times, and several other matters connected with their current level of alert. Although she was trained to respond to rapidly changing events like these – indeed she'd been selected because of her exemplary response in simulated situations just like this – she couldn't help feeling a deep sense of the gravity of this situation.

Quadrant 4 was the science sector. That had seemed less relevant when this mission began, because she and her team were supposed to be working in isolation, sole guardians of the Earth as the terraforming took place. When she'd read the briefing notes for a Tier 10 alert, she'd been shocked to discover the real purpose of her own bunker.

Dixia Cheng was also known as the 'Underground City'. It was a network of tunnels constructed under Beijing during the 1970s and open to the public for several years until it was closed for 'renovation'. This entire, massive facility had been hiding in open view. Unknown to the citizens above, it had been extended, fortified, upgraded, and secured for some future event, and all of this had gone on in open sight.

She was accustomed to assimilating all manner of difficult data quickly, efficiently and dispassionately, but, in spite of that, the information in Xiang's briefing notes made her gasp. Xiang – who had seen friends imprisoned and executed and comrades tortured and maimed – couldn't believe the secret that had been concealed from all of the staff in her

Quadrant. The underground facility of which she was Custodian in Dixia Cheng, Beijing, housed enough human and animal embryos to repopulate the entire planet twice over.

Chapter Six

Exhaustion

James was exhausted and weak. He'd gone from being an integral part of a top secret project to 'the enemy' in just a matter of hours and the bruises and cuts on his body told him that he really wasn't welcome in the bunker now.

The security guards who'd questioned and tormented him seemed to show a horrible spite and contempt that he simply hadn't detected before his capture. He felt as though somebody had flicked a switch and all of a sudden these regular people had become contaminated with the vitriol and hatred of somebody else altogether. He could tell that they were not acting on their own initiative – or even 'just following orders'. He was sure that those pulsating lights in their necks that he and Amy had spotted earlier were responsible for whatever was happening here. There was a definite and strong red pulse there now, it had happened since events had taken a dramatic turn in the Control Room, directly after the 20:00 briefing there.

James knew the game – he'd been working with the military long enough. He had to keep the interrogation process going as long as he could, to maintain the suspicion that he might know something vital. Once they believed they'd extracted all useful information from him, the chances were that he'd be disposed of in some way. The best he could hope for was the BioFiltration Area, but bearing in mind that the last thing he'd just seen in the Control Room was the switching off of life support systems in that area, it was not looking good.

Dazed and weary, James's mind forced itself into action. His survival depended on him thinking clearly. They'd left him alone in a holding cell now. Still the intimidation continued with the lights turned up far too bright. He had to close his eyes tight and turn towards the wall to give himself the space and focus to think.

When you're in a tight corner, you need to work through the options very quickly and thoroughly. This is what he and Amy had done all those years ago, when under terrible and immediate threat of violence.

'What are the options here?' James asked himself.

He guessed that Amy had been apprehended. He had no idea what had happened to her after that. All of the civilians would be dead within an hour or so, now that the BioFiltration Area had been effectively sabotaged on Kate's orders. So far, it wasn't looking good. Any hope of help was looking limited and even if he managed to escape, where would they go? If they stepped beyond the bunker doors, they'd succumb to the darkness outside – although Amy and the child had been fine. That was interesting, he'd not really thought about that before. How had Amy and her daughter done that?

Could it be anything to do with the pulsating lights in their necks? Amy's light was blue, his was blue, but the lights in the necks of all the other bunker staff – as far as he'd managed to observe so far – were red.

What was the difference?

He and Amy seemed immune to whatever it was that was controlling the other bunker staff. Amy had been immune from the darkness beyond the bunker doors. If only he could get a closer look at her daughter. If she had a blue light in her neck, maybe that was the secret to being able to beat the darkness outside? But how would you even see out there, even if you could avoid going into stasis once you'd been exposed?

He'd have to park these thoughts, they were interesting, but not useful right now. His only hope, it seemed to him, was the boy – Dan. And there was the other child who came in with Amy – where was she? Neither of those seemed to be a very good prospect. Surely the youngsters would be apprehended quite soon now. Kate wouldn't tolerate children in this environment. They'd probably end up the same as the rest of their family, currently dying slowly in the BioFiltration Area.

It was clear to James what needed to be done. His body ached, he was bruised, hurt and tired. But he was still alive. He'd exaggerated how hurt he'd been to buy himself this thinking time. They'd be back shortly to start their bullying and questioning again. They'd give him just enough time to recover, but they'd be back, they weren't finished yet.

No, it was quite clear to him now, nobody was going to come and save him. He'd have to use the few advantages that he had. The light was ridiculously bright but he was used to it. When the guards re-entered the room, it would take them a few vital seconds to adjust their eyes as the lights were normalized. He'd given the impression that they'd hurt him more than they had. Yes, he was sore, wounded and aching, but he could still run and fight if he had to.

The doors opened suddenly and James knew exactly what he had to do. He rushed at the guards before they even had a moment to adjust to the new lighting levels and see where James was in the room. He caught them completely by surprise. As he'd faced the wall with his eyes shut, he knew that effectively, he was about to make his bid for freedom completely blind.

He was going to do four things. He needed to focus: four things, one after the other, no pauses or hesitation.

First, the minute the doors opened, navigating by sound alone, he would rush directly at the guards, with all the force that he could muster.

Secondly, and probably with only partial vision at that time, he would grab a weapon which the guards would be holding roughly at waist level.

Third, he would fire it immediately to buy time and create panic among anybody else in the area.

By this time he should have recovered enough sight to figure out where to run.

So fourth, find the exit, fire wildly, and run for your life.

Ahead

I wish I could get Doctor Pierce in a room for five minutes and just ask him a few basic questions. I keep being given these snatches of information, but I never seem to get the full picture. It's like he's giving me individual pieces to a jigsaw when all I really want is the box with the picture on the front so that I can see what the finished thing looks like.

I quickly run through the information that he's given me. He doesn't seem to know about Nat for starters. That doesn't tally with what Nat is telling me. She hates him and blames him for whatever happened to her. Yet just a few moments ago he referred to her as if she's dead. Is he messing with me here? He thinks I think that Nat is dead. So that would explain that, maybe he's covering himself, just to be sure.

The best policy for now is to keep Nat hidden from him, so that we maintain that advantage at least. And where is Doctor Pierce? Where is he broadcasting from? He seems to have some 'access all areas' control. Presumably he can use security cameras and the like. But he still seems to think that I am the key, and Nat too by the sound of it. What is it about Nat and me that makes us central to all of this?

Okay, enough of the questions Dan, it's time for action. I was able to get the gist of what Doctor Pierce was saying in his main broadcast, and similarly, Nat seems to have been able to tune her ears into what Doctor Pierce was saying to me among the bedlam of all these voices and screens. Why didn't somebody leave the remote control somewhere where we could find it?

I might be leaping to conclusions here, but I reckon that the faces on the three screens are the Custodians of the other Quadrants. It would make sense. Kate must be our Custodian, she seems to be in charge here. I'm guessing that Magnus is the smaller guy on the screens in front of me. He looks more like he might be into technology, and the other guy looks like he lifts weights and can handle a bit of

THE SECRET BUNKER: THE FOUR QUADRANTS

manual labour. Yes, Magnus must be the geek type …
I can recognize 'my people' a mile away.

So Magnus is Quadrant 3. He has a faint yellow
light in his neck. It's not glowing at the moment, it
seems dormant. I'll need to remember that, it might
mean that he's working with Kate. Great, now how
do we communicate with him?

Nat starts to speak, her mind must be racing too.

'Dan, remember the buttons in the lifts?' she
begins.

I certainly do. I think Nat is heading where I'm
heading on this one.

'What Pierce said about needing my DNA …'

Interesting, she clearly dislikes this man, she's
dropping the 'Doctor' now.

'He doesn't know I'm here with you, so you
already have my DNA – it's me! I reckon if we use
the lifts, touch the weird buttons at the top together,
then press the buttons with the numbers on, it'll take
us to the other Quadrants.'

Okay, that's not quite the leap I made, Nat is way
ahead of me. If I'm going to be the hero that Doctor
Pierce seems to think I am, I'll have to get a lot
smarter and a lot quicker by the look of it. And Nat is
already ahead of me in those departments. I'm not so
sure.

'It makes sense,' Nat continues. 'In fact we may
not even need the lift, the Transporters might do it.'

'I don't know where I was before, but I'd
transported somewhere else that looked just like this
… it must have been one of the other Quadrants!'

Okay, I'm warming to this idea now.

'We need to find Mum and that James guy
though,' I interrupt, cutting Nat off in full flow. 'I

thought we'd agreed that?'

Nat pauses. It's funny being our age, because we still have that 'kid thing' where you want to rush at everything now, this minute, as soon as possible. But a wiser voice is there now too. It must be maturity intervening, because as much as we want to try out Nat's idea and meet Magnus, we know in our hearts that we must take care of the people closest to us first.

'So,' I begin, 'Comms-Tabs first like Doctor Pierce suggested, then we find Mum or that guy James she was with, and try to re-group.'

Nat nods in agreement.

'Then we hook up with Magnus,' I finish.

'And do whatever we can to sort out these drones,' Nat adds. 'This is not quite the reunion I was expecting Dan!'

I know what she means. We've barely had time to say 'Hello'. Now here we are trying to save the other Quadrants from a drone attack. I haven't even seen a real drone before, let alone stopped an attack by one. Still, follow the plan, Dan. Keep moving forwards, you know the next steps.

Magnus can help and if I can find Mum or Dad, even better, we can solve this together.

Nat and I head for the Weaponry Room which I've seen before, but now I know I'm looking for something called Comms-Tabs. I wonder for a moment if we should take some weaponry – will it come in useful at some point? I've had one of those guns pointed at me in this place; you don't stop to ask questions when you can see the small, red dot of a laser targeting system resting on your forehead. It seems laughable to even consider this – what would

Nat and I even do with a weapon? But she's ahead of me already and she goes immediately for a small, handheld unit, which looks a bit like a heavy duty stapler.

'What are we going to do Nat, staple them to the wall?' I ask, wondering if now is an appropriate time for humour. Nat smiles. It seems that now *is* a good time for humour. She chuckles, then says, 'I've seen one of these things in action. They're nasty and painful little critters.'

'They're like tasers,' she continues, looking at it in her hand. 'They give you a sharp and nasty stun, and they can knock you back for quite some time.'

Those words hang in the air again. What was Nat doing that resulted in her being around when one of these things was being used?

'I sound like I'm some sort of expert, I'm really not!' she laughs, and the mood lightens. It's so good having Nat back, it's like we just picked up where we left off, there's so much I want to ask her, but our connection has been immediate, even though we've been apart for so long.

She navigates her way around this area with ease and Nat knows exactly what the Comms-Tabs are. They just peel off and stick to the palm of your hand. Nat raises her hand towards her mouth and speaks into hers. I hear her voice in front of me and from a secondary source, but I'm not sure how, it's not coming out of a speaker as far as I can tell.

'Clever things these,' says Nat. 'I've never used them myself before but I've seen them used by other people. The guards I mean.'

Again, a hint of a story as yet untold. Soon Nat, we'll have time soon.

'I'm not entirely sure, but they seem to hook in on that first test, so yours and mine are now connected. We can talk to each other, and I suggest we take a few more in case we hook up with Mum or anybody else who can help.

'You don't receive the message via a speaker or an earpiece though; it seems to transmit the message directly to your brain, like it bypasses your ear drum and skips straight to the bit where the brain translates the message. Incredible stuff. I saw the guards using them – I wasn't quite sure how they worked, they seemed to be talking to themselves, like a fancy Bluetooth system.'

This kit is amazing. We both take a few of the Comms-Tabs so we have spares and we both take two of the taser devices as they're quite compact and fit in a pocket. It feels like we're getting 'tooled up' as they do in the movies. I hope we don't mess it up. Knowing my luck, right at the crucial moment I'll taser myself.

'Okay, we're good to go!' says Nat, and we head out of the Weaponry Room, into the curving corridor and towards the lift. When we're in the lift, we look at each other and smile. We know that we must find Mum first. But we've just got to try out Nat's theory.

Nat puts her hand on the panel with the weird markings. The lift jolts, just like it did when I tried it the first time. I place my hand on the panel while Nat's is still there. Nothing happens.

Nat moves her hand, initially in disappointment, but when she does, the lift jolts again. Incredibly, we are then surrounded by what I can only describe as an amazing haze of lights. Each of the edges of the lift illuminates, emitting a wonderful array of colours.

Nat presses the button marked '1' but the lift doesn't move. Instead, the wonderful patterns of light fill the lift, then everything stops and we appear to be where we were when we started. Only the doors open, and standing in front of us is the man called Magnus.

22:07 Quadrant 4: Dixia Cheng, Beijing

Xiang made sure that her bunker staff were on task and that the drones were being fully monitored, then stepped out of the Control Room to give herself some time to think and reflect. She was stunned to learn that her facility housed thousands, maybe even millions, of embryos, human and animal, and she could barely contemplate why that would be.

She knew the basics of the Genesis 2 project, but only since she'd received Tier 10 access in the light of the drone attack had the full responsibility dawned upon her. There were four bunkers – the four Quadrants of the Genesis 2 project – so she and her team were not alone in this.

Xiang was a scientist, but also a soldier and a leader. Her exceptional skills and ability in her field of expertise had resulted in her being courted at a very young age by the military, or at least an organization which appeared to be military in nature.

She was one of a new generation of synthetic biologists and geneticists, a deeply controversial role which resulted in furious accusations of 'playing God' and 'toying with life'. Much as animal testing had been condemned, so was her work in the private sector, to such an extent that she had tired of being hounded by the medical press and persecuted by the public.

It had been a relief to be approached by the military – or whoever they were – and to be able to progress her work in peace and with full funding. She believed in the good of what she was doing.

Xiang understood that with science came responsibility, but her genuine belief was that her work could help humanity, not threaten it. She didn't need to seek a full briefing about why this bunker held these embryos. This was a project that she'd been working on, but all of the teams involved had been isolated, much like the four bunkers were now. So they knew enough to play their part, but not enough to see the full picture.

Xiang's work had facilitated the creation of these embryos, through a system which allowed genetic replication on an industrial scale. She had facilitated what was – in effect – a factory for creating new life. Playing God? She knew that it was a close thing, but she couldn't actually create new life yet, only generate it from existing life. It was the next step in the process where the lines became truly blurred to her. It would have caused riots if it had ever become known by the press or public.

But the motivation was a good one. In the event of a global catastrophe – or a situation which wiped out all life on Earth – we had the ability to start all over again, to replace the lives that had been lost. Xiang didn't know what might cause that: nuclear war, environmental catastrophe, disease, asteroid collision – threats to the planet could come in any shape or form. So if the results of her work were secured somewhere in this bunker facility right now, something must be threatening the life on this planet.

From her point of view, it was theoretical work: she had proven it in the laboratory and in limited numbers. Who had taken her work and actually used it to create a factory for new animal and human life on such a large scale? As Xiang pondered these questions, she was unaware that in the days ahead her unique skills would be used to make an even more amazing discovery. It would be Xiang who finally unravelled the truth about Dan and Nat.

Chapter Seven

Change

The matrix of satellite sentinels waited patiently above the clouds. In an instant a bright, orange light shot out from fifty of the larger satellites which marked the key axis intersections in this vast grid. The orange light appeared to leap from satellite to satellite, linking them up so that the Earth was surrounded by a massive, enveloping orange web.

Beyond the web was the sun, the moon and the rest of space. Inside the web was an orb of blackness where nothing could be seen or heard. Once the web was fully completed between the hundreds of satellites which orbited above the planet, there was a moment of stillness.

Then, simultaneously, the satellites received new data. Spiral doors opened like a shutter on a camera, and large, long and heavy Shards emerged, like the spines on a vast, metallic sea urchin. In unison, the Shards lit up, sending an intense beam towards the Earth.

Anybody on Earth, if they'd been able to view this

process, might have been fleetingly alarmed by what was going on. It looked like hundreds of satellites orbiting the Earth were firing torpedo-like missiles towards the surface. The Shards were different colours, some blue, some green, others purple and the remainder yellow.

This was the next stage of the terraforming process, it was time now for the darkness to subside and for new life to be breathed into the planet. Each of the Shards carried different elements that the Earth would need to rejuvenate; it was a vastly accelerated process that could undo the harm that had been inflicted on the planet, mostly in the past two hundred years.

The entire biosphere of the planet – lithosphere, hydrosphere and atmosphere – was being healed, the Earth's ecosystems recalibrated and balanced once again. The blue Shards were to reinvigorate the atmosphere, cleansing it of deadly carbon emissions and pollutants left there by Man. These Shards hovered above the Earth's surface in the place where the skies once were – and where they would return shortly. If the project was a success.

The green Shards were to nourish the seas, restoring them to the way they were when they were originally placed in the care of humans and breathing new life into them. These devices took up positions within the world's deepest waters, suspended and still in the darkness there.

The yellow Shards bore far into the Earth's crust like powerful drills, altering the geology of the planet, rebalancing the processes that had depleted resources through mining and drilling. Humans were unaware that oil, gas and coal are a crucial part of the Earth's balanced ecosystem until it was far too late. Future generations would source power in different ways, using technology that could barely be imagined.

Finally, the purple Shards circulated in seemingly random patterns, weaving just above the surface and releasing nano and biotechnology into every part of the Earth's environment. It was these undetectable and microscopic guardians which would continue this process of renewal once the world had been reawoken.

This was the Genesis 2 project: many years in the planning, incredible in its vast scope and incomprehensible to anybody but the most advanced scientists and technologists in terms of its delivery. In the stillness of space, as the entire planet slept below, and the four bunkers began to fight with each other in a power struggle that was supposed to have been totally improbable – impossible even – there was nobody to ask the obvious question.

Who was it that started this process and who now had control of it?

Rescue

Amy rushed towards Simon, her senses confused by what was going on. One minute he was shooting her, the next he was healing her, then she decided to trust him, and now he had just turned off the machines which contained three members of her family. Simon was taken aback by the speed at which she threw herself at him.

'Whoa!' he shouted. 'It's fine, relax. I just saved them all!'

Amy was still hostile, defensive and unsure. 'I

know it looks a bit basic,' he said, 'but I just had to remove the power source. Kate was actually using the machines to shut down the life support element. To stop that, we have to shut down the power completely.'

Amy looked at him, she was still unsure, and he sensed that more explanation was needed.

'The machines were actually interfering with their biology, they're now on their own, existing without interference from the machines.'

His face changed and Amy detected bad news was about to follow.

'We need to get them out of there and make sure that they're okay though,' Simon explained. 'Just pray that the machines haven't done too much damage.'

As if on cue, Mike's body jolted as if he was awakening rudely from a dream. It was very sudden and it immediately took Amy's attention away from her altercation with Simon. The other bodies in the cocoons started to jolt too, and one by one their eyes began to open. All but David and Harriet, whose bodies remained still and lifeless as the adults woke slowly and confused around them.

'I think the children have less resistance to whatever these things were doing to them,' Simon volunteered, recognizing the seriousness of the situation straight away.

'We need to get them out fast.'

Amy didn't need another cue. Simon took David out of his unit, and Amy helped Harriet. Both bodies were limp and lifeless. Amy was desperate – around her she had the sensation of the adults slowly waking and coming around from their deep sleep, but in front of her, two of her children appeared to be dead.

'Massage their hearts!' commanded Simon. 'Use CPR.'

Amy cursed that she couldn't remember exactly what to do – how many compressions and how many breaths was it? Either Simon knew what he was doing or he was just getting on with it. Amy pressed down on Harriet's chest as hard as she dared. She was still so small and fragile, not like Dan who had left childhood long behind and was built more like Mike these days.

To her right she heard David draw breath. 'I've got him back!' shouted Simon. 'He's okay!'

Amy pushed down on Harriet's chest, she breathed into her mouth and she watched her tiny chest rise as she did so. No signs of life. She carried on for a few minutes longer, desperate to revive her youngest child.

At the point when the majority of people would have given up, when most people would have decided to stop through tiredness, exhaustion and a realization that it was useless, Amy found deep within her the power that had driven her forward all of those years previously when she'd taken a chance and shot James.

She put her hands together and pushed down with all the pressure that she could muster, deep into Harriet's chest. It was a massive, forceful, even desperate push.

There was a crack as one of Harriet's ribs broke from the force.

Then Harriet jolted suddenly and sharply drew in her first breath. And as she did so, four armed guards swarmed into the BioFiltration Area, pointing their weapons directly at Amy and Simon.

Burned

Essentially, the two children got on well most of the time, but the parents had a very real concern about one of them. It began as a gut feeling the first time that the wooden block had been used in the unprovoked violent attack. But it was confirmed a few months later.

It was bath time. Usually this was one of the highlights of the day, when the two children – now toddling – would rush towards the bathroom, eager to get into the water together and to start playing with the toys.

On this particular evening, all was as normal. She was reading her book, perched on the side of the towel chest, while the two children played amicably.

Then, without warning, one of them picked up a pouring jug, moved towards the hot tap and filled it with water. The scalding water was then poured over the other child, who hadn't even realized what was going on.

In the wails and confusion that followed as she tried to comfort the scalded child and placed a cold, wet flannel over the red raw area, an unnerving thought came to her.

Was there something wrong with this other child or was this just an accident of childhood experimentation? She would have put it down as a youthful accident if it weren't for the sight that was confronting her now.

The child who had poured the water was sitting alone in the bath completely unperturbed by what had just happened.

In fact, right at this moment, as she did her best to

comfort and soothe the injured child, the other was just sitting there, looking at her and smiling.

Breakout

'Magnus?' I ask, knowing that it must be him.

I look at the yellow light in his neck. The people surrounding him have them too. They're visible, but not pulsating now. Just like Mum's and James's. He seems to be safe.

'Dan?' he queries. 'And who's this?'

'This is my sister Nat,' I reply. 'Only we don't have time to chat.'

'Fancy helping us?' Nat asks, and I'm ready to challenge that when I reconsider my response and think, 'Why not?'

Judging by how worried Magnus looked in that video message that I was watching only minutes ago, I reckon he's as keen as we are right now to stop those drones.

'Of course,' replies Magnus, 'just tell me what to do. Doctor Pierce said to help you.'

Interesting, he's fine with Doctor Pierce. Nat seems to be the only one with the problem.

'Put this on,' says Nat, handing him a Comms-Tab, 'and take this too.'

She hands him one of the stun devices.

'Point this way and press that button. It only stuns, it doesn't kill.'

I'm pleased Nat mentioned which way to point it. I really would have shot myself if she hadn't given Magnus that information.

'Now let's try something else,' she says, indicating that we all need to be in the lift.

Her hand reaches the pad in the lift before mine, and interestingly, this time, the lights come on without me having to touch anything. I wonder if this thing remembers us, like the first time we both have to activate it, but after that we can do it on our own – a bit like the credit cards that Mum and Dad get in the post.

Nat's thinking the same thing, and she looks at me and smiles. She presses the button marked '1' – for our Quadrant I hope, not Level 1 – and once again the wonderful lights appear, then fade out again once we have been transported.

I don't think Magnus is even aware of what happened. I think he's expecting the door to open on the same floor that we just left, having enjoyed a lovely light display in between. But if Nat and I are right – and I know what she's thinking about this – we just transported back to Quadrant 1 and when this lift door opens we're going to be on Level 1 in our own bunker. Kate's territory.

We both grasp our stun devices tightly. I make sure mine is pointing the right way, and Nat shows Magnus how the Comms-Tab works. 'If we get separated, talk into this, we're all linked,' she instructs. 'Apparently they can't monitor our conversations at the moment, but they might be able to later, so be careful what you say.

'Or so Pierce says!' she almost spits out.

Magnus is a man after my own heart. He immediately loves the technology and gets it, even if he doesn't fully understand it yet. Amazing how our beliefs have expanded to fit the incredible world that we have created with technology.

In medieval times you'd have been burned at the

stake if you'd been found with one of these devices, but nowadays whatever we can imagine, we can create. So why wouldn't we have 'peel and stick' communications devices which link directly into our hearing receptors?

'Ready?' asks Nat. She's about to open the lift door.

When we step out onto this floor we can be seen on the cameras; they'll know that we're here. The doors slide open, and we're stunned by what happens next.

As the doors open, a bloody and wrecked looking James runs through them, taking cover from two guards who are firing at him and chasing him. He's just as surprised to see us.

Nat and I move fast, we know it's time to use the stun devices. But Magnus beats us to it. Fire one, fire two and both guards are down. Nat and I look at each other and we look at Magnus. I like this man.

James is still all business. 'Your family, quickly, we need to get your family.'

James looks a mess, goodness knows what has happened to him, I've never seen somebody in such a dreadful physical state before. Not in real life at least.

'This way!' shouts James, and we all follow, stun devices at the ready.

James has a weapon and seems to know how to use it. Now that's handy. The alert has been sounded and the incessant siren is really quite oppressive in the bunker's long corridor.

We reach the BioFiltration Area but the door is already open. Just a split second to take this in. Four guards, Mum, Dad, David, and Harriet who is making a terrible wailing sound and holding her chest. She's giving the siren a run for its money.

The only people who don't belong here are the guards. They're too slow for us, it's a bit like a quick draw from a cowboy film, and we stun them before they can shoot us.

I like these tasers. You don't even have to aim them really accurately, they sense the target, lock and fire. And I'm only stunning them, so I can live with that.

All of a sudden it's like a massive, surprise family reunion. All my family is here: Dad sees Nat, Nat sees everybody else, Mum sees all of the kids back in one place again. For a moment it's all a bit much.

But we're not out of this yet. Above the sirens I can hear a noise that puts all of us in very immediate peril. It's the approaching sound of stomping boots as a large and armed team of security guards moves urgently along the bunker corridor, intent on finishing us all off for the last time.

Chapter Eight

22:14 Quadrant 2: Balaklava Bay, Crimea

Viktor had removed himself from the Control Room to find some temporary peace and quiet from the constant buzz of activity. He was a man more pleased by being in nature than in an artificial environment like this bunker.

He'd been selected for this role because of his very extensive and distinguished experience in the field of biotechnology. Like the other Custodians in the bunkers, Viktor also had a military background, though his was rather more informal in nature.

Much of science can be controversial and problematical, particularly when working on projects for private companies which have a duty to report most of what is going on to shareholders.

When Viktor's teams began to make innovative breakthroughs in the areas of green and red biotechnology, they started to garner unwanted attention from the media and campaign groups.

At about that time, a former contact arranged a discreet meeting to inform Viktor that the military was extremely interested in the work that he was doing. Or at least they appeared to be the military, Viktor could tell that it was certainly governmental in nature. He would be able to continue working, fully funded, but away from the glare of the public eye.

Viktor had first got to know this military contact when he was a much younger man, just out of university and returning to a country whose politics were in turmoil. It was there that Viktor had become a master of leadership and strategy in guerrilla warfare and he had built up an excellent reputation and track record as a commander. He had also got a very dark reputation as a man who got things done – whatever the cost in terms of human life.

After order and legal rule had returned to his country, Viktor threw himself into his scientific work where he demonstrated as much flair and innovation as he had on the battlefield.

Viktor had remarkable leadership abilities in the field of biotechnology and was directing multiple project strands in a number of areas. Put very simply, he had facilitated several cutting-edge breakthroughs in numerous branches of his specialist area.

It was Viktor's teams who had developed a system

for micro-propagating genetically modified crops without the need for natural light. You could now create vast arable farms in hostile farming environments. His teams had taken that work one step further and been able to grow arable crops in seawater, a preemptive response to fast rising sea levels.

But it was in the field of red biotechnology – or genetic manipulation – that Viktor had experienced his biggest breakthrough. His teams had stumbled across it by accident, but it had troubled Viktor ever since he'd sat in the briefing room to hear the full results of the exhaustive studies. Whilst working on a genetic manipulation project focused on trans-humanization – the enhancement of human beings – Viktor had discovered a process by which this could be achieved remotely.

The military applications of this were extensive. You could create whole armies of soldiers – remove any genetic disorders or physical weaknesses – then control elements such as intellectual, physical, and psychological capacities to forge warriors who were almost incapable of error or failure. Viktor could manufacture the strongest, most intelligent and efficient soldier ever known to humankind, all of it via a laboratory.

Was it 'playing God?' Viktor didn't know. But as a man who knew from his own personal experiences the necessity of using huge force at certain times and in particular situations, he understood the value to the military of such a discovery.

He just hoped that it would be used for good.

Change

As each one of the hundreds of satellites circling the planet released its vast, glowing Shards and projected its healing energy through the darkness, a change began to take place below.

Where once it was black, thick and impenetrable, minute by minute it started to take on a hue that had become less black and much more blue.

There was change taking place beneath this blanket which had been wrapped around the world to help to cure it of its diseases. Billions of life forms continued to slumber – on the surface and in the oceans – unaware of the changes that were taking place around them.

What was occurring was a highly advanced terraforming process which had been carefully balanced to enrich the planet once again where it had been plundered and left bereft. This was about replenishing, regenerating and rebuilding. It was a positive process, one of growth and creation. But it could also be adapted for other purposes too.

The advanced technology which was healing the Earth could also be used to destroy it.

Terraforming is a process which is deployed to manipulate a planet's atmosphere, temperature, surface topography, and ecology to make it just like Earth. Or in the case of the Genesis 2 project, to recreate the Earth as it once was, before it was damaged by the industrial and wartime activities of Man.

But what if the planet didn't need to be like Earth? When men created the term 'terraforming' it was a sign of their vanity that they used it to create an

Earth-like atmosphere and environment. Not everybody needed to create a place like Earth. Not everybody needed an atmosphere or environment like our planet. And not everybody needed a planet with life forms on its surface.

Sanctuary

This is almost the moment I've been waiting for – all of my family are in the same room together at last. Harriet is quite obviously in some discomfort. Who knows what happened here, but she seems to be in considerable pain. Mum looks exhausted and sore, in fact she doesn't even look like Mum, she's changed her appearance so much since I last caught sight of her. Dad and David just look dazed, they don't really seem to have a grasp of what's going on. They're vague in their behaviour and, although they recognize us, they don't seem to be fully aware or conscious.

There's another man in the room too, next to Mum and with David. I assume he's friendly because Mum accepts his presence here. I'll go with her judgement, but he looks familiar and I'm struggling to place his face. I can sense that Nat feels that familiarity too.

There's not much time for introductions now. The approaching heavy footfall means that we have very little time to take the initiative over the approaching guards.

I'm quite surprised by what I do next. I step in and take control. And nobody stops me. In fact, they all seem to agree with me. 'We need to get to the lift!' I shout, 'But we're going to have to fire our way through. Everybody who has a weapon will need to provide a shield, but we need to get to the end of the corridor and then to the lift entrance before they start to send reinforcements.'

I still have a spare stun device which I hand over to Mum who seems to be the best person to take it right now. The man she's with has a weapon, as does James, who looks terrible with all his cuts and bruises. Nat, Magnus and I have stun devices. We're well kitted out between us.

It's funny to think that only two days earlier we were touring this place as holiday makers. It's turned into some really extreme holiday experience, not the sort of thing you'd book through your travel agent.

The other people in the room appear useless. It pains me to say it but even Dad is so vague that he's not going to be a lot of help to us in this fight. We need to get him, David, Harriet and the people who worked as guides in the bunker safely to that lift. Nat and I can then transport everybody back to Magnus's Quadrant which Kate doesn't appear to have access to at the moment.

Whatever is 'special' about Nat and me is the key to this. I haven't a clue what it is yet, and I certainly don't feel special in any way, but I'm going to go with the information that I've got for now.

We position ourselves as best we can along the corridor. It's not a great place for a confrontation, as there are very few areas to take cover. I'm no military strategist but I know the basics. I need to hide where they can't shoot me but I can shoot them.

I'm nervous and breathing fast, it seems incredible that I'm here and involved in this right now. If it was a dream I wouldn't be surprised, but my senses are so alert I know that this is definitely for real.

It's good news for us that Kate's security teams obviously don't think that our ramshackle army is any threat whatsoever, so there are only six guards in the team that comes to apprehend us. That puts the odds in our favour, though they have proper weapons – we mainly have stun devices.

We have the advantage, so are first to fire. They're not expecting us, so we stun three of them immediately. 'Get ready to run!' I shout to Dad, who is with the civilians around the corner, on standby to run for their lives.

He's carrying Harriet too, but he still seems completely out of it. He can see what's going on here, but he just isn't engaged in it.

The guards return fire. This is scary, it's very fast and intense and it's extremely difficult to tell what's going on. I hope we're stunning these people rather than hurting them. I've seen what has been done to James, but I don't want to be hurting anybody. I'm still hoping that we can fix this like a playground altercation – just shake hands, apologize and move on – but the returning weapon fire is suggesting otherwise.

Nat's really into this, she's firing her stun device like she's playing a fairground game and another of the guards drops to the floor. The remaining two are retreating now and it's Mum who actually signals that we should start to move forward towards the lift.

Normally she can't even survive a few laps of a console motor racing game, but now here she is, stun gun in hand, waving us all forward. Wow, I'm impressed. I'm guessing we have some catching up to do, because in that photo I spotted in the Control Room she was wearing a military uniform.

I've never seen her like this before. I know that she can manage a unit of school children, get their lunch boxes packed up, and have them all dressed and out of the house by 8.45 a.m. But she's really in control here, firing her weapon alongside Nat and helping us press forward along the corridor.

All the time the alert sirens are sounding loudly, it can't be long until reinforcements arrive. We're almost at the lift and I think we're going to make it when a laser beam fires just by my ear and hits one of the bunker staff behind me. I don't even know these people, yet this woman only has time to give a small cry before she's thrown back onto the floor, with shocking force.

The familiar looking man who's next to Mum goes to help her, but indicates that she's dead. 'Can't you use your machine on her?' yells Mum, still firing at the two guards who are slowly retreating ahead of us.

'It heals damaged tissue, it can't bring her back,' he replies. 'I'm sorry, we'll have to leave her.'

I've never seen a dead body before and I'm scared and frightened by the speed and force of what just happened. To be honest with you, I haven't done much in this corridor battle so far and I'm a bit stunned by everything happening around me. But now I feel angry for this woman – I don't know what's going on in this bunker yet, but I do know that I want more than anything right now to get all of these people into that lift, and back to the safety of Magnus's Quadrant.

I don't know what comes over me. Whatever it is, I think it got to Nat and Mum already, but a rage surges through me and I fire my stun device with absolute precision towards the two remaining guards.

I'm yelling as I do, but I find both targets and they slump to the floor. I'm still yelling when I realize that the firing has stopped and everybody is looking at me in stunned silence.

'Nice shooting Dan!' Nat breaks the silence. 'All those computer games have paid off.'

I'm concerned about how normal this seems to her. Nat isn't fazed at all by what's going on here, she takes all of this violence in her stride. I even think that she was quite excited by the fight we've just had.

We can hear the thudding of more boots as the reinforcements make their way up the corridor from the opposite direction, so there's no time to talk now. We bundle ourselves into the lift. I hesitate to call it a lift because, as we now know, it's so much more than that. Maybe 'transporter' is a better word, or 'shuttle'.

We're all in and the door closes just as the first blast of hostile fire shoots along the corridor. The light array begins to fill the lift signalling that the Transporter is activated, and the doors open at our new destination. We've managed to escape to Quadrant 3. For now, we have sanctuary.

Chapter Nine

Psychologist

It's very difficult to get a diagnosis that your young child is a sociopath. And who would want that particular diagnosis for their own child? But after the scalding water incident in the bath, both parents had an uneasy feeling about this child.

They had searched everywhere for clues and information. How do you describe the violent actions of a young child? Are they random experiments, carried out without thought of consequence? Or are they calculated and planned, the expression of an evil mind?

So, with their child at the very young age of only three years old, they found themselves sitting in the psychologist's office discussing whether there could be something wrong with this particular toddler. As all parents would be, they were scared to learn the answer.

The psychologist listened attentively and nodded with sympathy as they retold the stories about the wooden brick and the scalding water. They held back about the incident involving the scissors. If she forgot to keep her sleeve pulled down fully you could still see the wound; it had been deep and painful. Whilst enjoying a simple art activity with the children, her sharp scissors had been grabbed from her hand when her attention was diverted and plunged deep into her wrist.

As parents, they could still not bring themselves to admit that incident to anybody. They felt shamed in some way, as if it was their fault, as if they were responsible for what this child was doing.

They spent some time with the psychologist, but she was adamant in her opinion. At three years old, you simply can't pigeonhole a child as being a 'sociopath'. If you do apply that label, they may become one anyway, simply because of the way that you treat them. So, for now, there was to be no help or support for them, they were on their own with this.

As parents, they knew that something wasn't right here, but as the psychologist had stressed, this matter would not be taken too seriously until the child was older. Certainly they would need to be attending school and old enough to be able to determine what is right and what is wrong.

As they thanked the psychologist for her time, she gave her husband a disappointed look. They had really needed some assistance here, this was the only cry for help that they felt they could make. And now the door was being closed on them. They were on their own.

With a child who was going to become deceitful, manipulative and a sickening murderer.

22:27 Quadrant 3: White Sulphur Springs, West Virginia

You can actually feel the sense of relief as the door opens onto a quiet, calm corridor where there are no sirens going off and no weapons being fired at us. I'm not sure if anybody even realized what just happened in the panic – they saw the lights in the lift of course, but I don't think they can tell that we just moved between bunkers.

I have to admit that I'm totally stunned by what Magnus says next: 'Welcome to West Virginia,' he says, 'you are all very welcome and safe in Quadrant 3.'

'West Virginia?'

Virtually everybody asks the same question at one time.

'Yes, Quadrant 3 is located underground in White Sulphur Springs, West Virginia,' Magnus continues. 'Don't ask me how we did it, but we appear to have just travelled well over three thousand miles in a matter of seconds!'

There's astonishment all around, but I think that we've all seen so much that's unfamiliar and out of place in the past forty-eight hours that we would believe anything right now. Members of Magnus's team arrive to greet us, and it's good to see guards and bunker staff who don't seem to want us dead, even though they all have those yellow lights in their necks – dormant for now, but potentially a future threat.

Mum's friend James and Harriet are in most need of help. Harriet seems to be in a bad way and James looks in need of some urgent medical attention. He was great in that fight we just had though, a real asset.

The other man who was helping David has taken a very obvious interest in the pads and buttons in the lift. I think he's trying to figure out how we just did what we did. I don't know this man yet, but Mum has vouched for him and he certainly helped us in the showdown we just had in Quadrant 1.

He puts his hand on the pad next to the unusual symbols, but nothing happens. Not even the jolt that Nat and I got when we tried it on our own. What is it about me and my twin that enables us to do something so cool in a place that we've never even been to before? I'd love to know, but I think that Doctor Pierce is going to be the one who sheds some light on that.

Magnus is clearly in charge right now, just as Kate had asserted her authority in her own bunker earlier that day. I instantly like Magnus, he's geeky, but he's also calm, reassuring and in control. I think he likes me too, he speaks very easily to me, he doesn't treat me like a kid, and I appreciate that. After all I just gave my first ever orders. And people even listened to me.

Magnus directs his team to take care of those who need it. I hug Dad, check in on David, and ask Mum about Harriet. She looks guilty and concerned, but reassures me that Harriet is okay, and that she probably has a broken rib.

Everybody who was in the BioFiltration Area is being taken to the MedLab for a full check over, just like I had when I was first found in Quadrant 1. That means that Dad, David, Harriet, the bunker staff and James are heading for the MedLab. The group in the cocoons still seem dazed to me – I was talking to Dad but he still isn't all there. There are hugs given and some reassurances, and that group splits off.

Magnus tries to get Mum to go to the MedLab but she refuses. She's talking to Nat, asking her what seem to be a million questions per second and making no progress at all. In the end she just gives up and holds her tightly, like she's never going to let her go. She cries and is overcome with emotion. Of course, Nat has an advantage over us, she knew that she was fine all the time when we thought she was dead. For Nat, this is a long anticipated reunion – not the resurrection that it is for us.

Magnus brings our thoughts back to business. 'Okay, we need to head for a Meeting Room everybody,' he begins. 'We have very little time here.

'The drones will begin to reach their targets very soon and, according to Doctor Pierce, Dan is going to be the one who helps us to stop them.

'Bearing in mind what you just did in that lift Dan, I think that's our clue as to how we're going solve this problem. Somehow you have a higher level of access.'

We're escorted along the corridors towards this

bunker's Control Room. The familiar looking man accompanies us, nobody seems to have challenged him yet, and I'm still wrestling with why I feel like I know him. Was he one of the tourism staff in the bunker? Did I see him when we were coming in two days earlier? I'm sure that's not it, I wish I could place him.

Although the layout is very different, whoever kitted out and transformed the Scottish bunker also did the same to this one. The look, feel and colour scheme is exactly the same, as is the technology. It's sleek, hi-tech, clean, ultra-modern and not like anything I've ever seen before.

The Meeting Room is businesslike but comfortable; it's very well lit and there are display screens at the far end. They show various bits of data, but it's the video feeds that grab my attention. They must be visuals of the drones – these maps are tracking the trajectories of their flight paths.

I can figure out what these screens are telling me and it doesn't take a genius to know what that number counting down in front of us is monitoring. We have very little time now until the first drone will strike this bunker.

22:42 Quadrant 1: Troywood, Fife

Kate surveyed the Control Room and noted with satisfaction that the attack plan appeared to be going well. The drones were launching at regular intervals and continued to do so, carrying their deadly packages to pre-designated targets. They were launching from an area in her own bunker facility which even she, as Custodian, didn't yet have access to. That would be resolved shortly.

Controlled by the device in her neck, as were all of those around her, she carried out the instructions that were transmitted directly to the receptors in her brain. She was furious about the debacle on the upper level. They had lost every civilian that had entered this bunker and several of her security staff had ended up in the MedLab as a result of their escape.

There were two deaths as well – and the woman who was supposed to have been shot dead in the BioFiltration Area was still alive. Deception and subterfuge, right under her nose, in her bunker.

What was troubling her more though was how they'd got away. She'd watched on the security cameras as the escape took place. She watched them all make their way into the lift. A few moments elapsed, the security guards opened the lift door and … it was empty. How did they do that? She was about to find out. From a secret location, via a source presently unknown to her, a new set of data arrived on her E-Pad. This data set would give her full access to the bunker, meaning that she and her teams would finally be able to reach the lower levels – the levels that only hours earlier she had believed didn't even exist – the levels where she assumed that the civilian group would be hiding.

The data would outline the full scope of her mission and the purpose of her bunker in the Genesis 2 project. It would give her access to information which the Custodians were never supposed to know. Information that they were never even meant to need.

Above the bunker in Quadrant 1, through metres of concrete and soil, the terraforming process continued, the Earth's hue now a dark blue. Inside the bunker she was about a receive a secure and encrypted message from the person orchestrating this present chaos – the person whose sabotage had resulted in the launching of scores of drones, each one fixated on its evil mission. The person whose destructive intentions extended far beyond the drone attack which was useful only in obliterating all opposition to the main objective.

The destruction of the other three bunkers was only the beginning. It would start with that, and the drones would begin their air strikes within minutes – a relentless and targeted assault on the bunkers hidden deep underground, and impregnable against nuclear attack. But not if you knew their exact location of course. And not if you knew their areas of weakness.

Kate moved to one of the meeting rooms, and adjusted the blinds so that she was alone and unobserved. Her E-Pad gave an electronic beep, and she entered a series of secure codes.

The screen immediately activated and a video feed of a man sitting at his desk appeared. She knew the face already, but the nameplate on his desk confirmed it if she'd had any doubt. It read 'Dr H. Pierce'.

PART TWO: RESISTANCE

Chapter One

Hacker

It was 6.19 a.m. and the student was mindful of an essay that needed to be submitted at 9 a.m. later that morning. But he was onto something far more interesting here. He'd been working on it for over a week in his bedroom, snatching whatever time he could after school and at the weekend.

At that time very few people had personal computers in their homes, but he'd managed to create a 'Frankenstein's monster' of a contraption in his bedroom. His parents were none the wiser. They just assumed that this was a passing phase, a teenage hobby which involved building some contrivance that looked not unlike a robot. If only they had known.

They were fortunate enough to have an ISDN line installed at home for his dad's work. ISDN stood for Integrated Services Digital Network, and at that time the few people who even knew that you could access the internet via your phone line would have given anything to achieve the speeds that could be obtained over this connection. ISDNs were in common use in the broadcasting industry in the 1990s, and his dad, a radio journalist, used the line to avoid him having to go into the office for early morning live radio hook-ups.

He'd sit at the breakfast table in his pyjamas, with a microphone in front of him, broadcasting to the entire country and taking mouthfuls of cornflakes in between interviews. At that time it was amazing stuff, but these days anybody could do exactly the same thing from the top of a mountain so long as they could get a few bars on their mobile device.

He'd soon realized that he could hijack his dad's ISDN at night, when it was never used, giving him access to speeds that most early surfers could only dream of. He had to be off the line by 7 a.m. ready for whatever interview his dad would be giving that morning to radio stations all over the country.

He reckoned he could have his essay knocked off by 8.30 a.m. and be in school for 8.50 a.m., particularly as he'd written a program to assemble most of the information that he needed automatically whilst he was working on this far more interesting project.

It would be a few years yet before institutions of learning understood that plagiarism was going to provide a constant challenge for teachers, lecturers, and examination boards, all intent on confirming the originality of academic endeavour. So he tapped away at his keyboard, working diligently through levels of code and security until, finally, he was in.

It was not so early in the history of the internet that Parliament had not had time to pass The Computer Misuse Act. He'd heard his dad talking about that one on the radio and as a younger teenager it was what had really got him interested in delving deeper into computers and the possibilities of the internet.

After obtaining the infamous 'Hacker's Manifesto' he'd been captivated, not because he wanted to do any damage or harm, but just because it was possible. It was like a battle between him and Them. 'Them' being any kind of authority: governments, banks, even his dad's broadcasting corporation. They all set themselves up as secure and impregnable, but they weren't – and they were misleading the public claiming that they were.

All he liked to do was to break in and just leave a little message. Like a message in a bottle. 'Managed to crack your security while you weren't looking. Take more care next time. I'm not here to do any damage – but the next person might be. Don't be so relaxed and complacent! Love, The Undertaker'. He liked that one, and it was a nod to his wrestling hero at the time.

It was mostly the problem solving that he enjoyed. Poring over code was a pleasure to him, completely absorbing, and it was so logical and predictable. You just had to spot the patterns. And he was onto one now. This one was a devil to crack, but he could see what they'd done and he was now able to unravel it. Just a little more … and … he was in!

An unfamiliar logo appeared on the screen. The graphics card on his home computer rig was extremely dodgy, but he could see that the image had been created for much more sophisticated systems than the one that he was presently using. It read 'The Global Consortium'.

Much of the documentation there looked fairly dull to his teenage self: paperwork about the formation of a worldwide group, mention of 'potential global catastrophe', and more paperwork dating back to 27 November 1983 when some important agreement was signed. He'd got the sense that this was really important, but that he'd need to delve much deeper into the additional levels of security which were protecting some of the more interesting looking documents. He'd left a wormhole into the system so that he could access it at any time, without being detected, and without having to go through the long hacking process which he'd just endured.

He could hear his dad's alarm going off in the next room now and knew that he'd have to shut down the ISDN so that it was ready for him when it was needed. Hopefully, nobody would spot the bill on that line, or they'd just assume his dad had been very busy with interviews.

He printed out the research information so that he could use it offline, rattled off his essay and managed to reach his completion target and have it handed in at school just in the nick of time. It took more time for the dot matrix printer to chug out the notes and there were plenty of paper jams in there for good measure.

'Should be an A or a B grade minimum,' he thought. In fact he was day-dreaming at his desk, thinking about the strategy he'd need to get into those other, more interesting, files, when there was an interruption from the Head Teacher in the middle of the lesson. There was a hushed conversation with the class teacher and a nod of assent, then the following request. 'Mike Tracy, go with the Head Teacher to his office please.' He'd been rumbled.

22:57 Quadrant 3: White Sulphur Springs, West Virginia

Magnus is a little bit out on his timings because we've ended up gaining a thirty minute advantage on the drones: thirty minutes in which to catch up with the latest information about what happened to Mum, Dad and the rest of the family and then to formulate a plan.

Mum can't stop holding Nat's hand, like she doesn't believe that she's really here and wants to make sure that she won't disappear again. Fair enough really I suppose. For me, Nat's reappearance is different. Of course I'm pleased, relieved, delighted, and all of the other things that I'm supposed to be. But I can tell that she feels it too. We're meant to be together.

I can't explain it, it's something bigger than me and I certainly don't understand it. When Nat and I are together, it enhances us – our thinking is clearer, our minds are sharper, our intelligence is greater. When I thought that Nat was dead, I was probably too young to explain it then, even though I was feeling that loss. I expressed it badly at school, by lashing out, by being hostile towards other kids, by having a short temper. Those were my 'difficulties' and I suppose it was just an inability to express that helplessness that I'd experienced after Nat went. Not the normal sense of grief and loss – it was more like a part of my own consciousness had died that day.

I can feel myself getting stronger and sharper all the time. It's like a surge through my veins I feel energized, awake, alive and alert. Dare I even use the word 'powerful'? Not in a dominant 'rule the world' kind of way. Just that, with Nat here, I feel that nothing can stop me. I've never experienced confidence and sureness like this before. I know that Nat is experiencing this too; she feels like she should be indulging Mum, but from the looks that she keeps giving me, I know that she's getting this power thing too.

I'm beginning to see how this is piecing together now, though I still can't explain it. There's something different about Nat and me. I can't even guess what it is, but it must be connected with us being twins and the changes that we're experiencing, now that we've been reunited. I'm guessing too, and I think that this is more than a hunch, that Nat's 'death' was engineered in some way. That incident – and the events in these bunkers – are linked. What we have to do now is to figure out how.

So here's what I've just learned. Dad, David and Harriet are fine. Harriet had a few ribs broken – by Mum of all people – but the MedLab team reported that she actually saved Harriet by doing that. They've used some amazing machine on Harriet and the ribs have been healed. She's now playing happily in the 'RecRoom'. I assume that's short for 'recreation'. See, I said I'm feeling sharper.

David and Dad just needed some coming round time. The stasis process had put them very deep under, it slowed their vital signs and, add to that Kate's attempt to slow them down to nothing, and that explains why Dad was so useless in that escape mission. Still, there's plenty of time to make up for it.

The other staff from the bunker are fine too, they're all going to be allowed to sit it out in what's now been designated a 'civilian area'. Basically, that means the RecRoom, the refectory and the dorms.

Mum had been quite badly wounded it would seem, but Simon has shown us this device he used to heal her and it emerges that Magnus is already familiar with this stuff. It's standard technology in the bunkers apparently. Magnus says that it will have been used on me already when I was in the MedLab. It can heal and cure, but it can't restore life. So it speeds up natural processes which would occur over time anyway. But it can't fix you when you're dead. Pity the Department of Health hasn't picked up on it yet. It's amazing technology, everybody in this room just seems to accept it without question. Except me. And Nat probably. I want to know where it comes from. Who makes stuff like this? This is amazing gadgetry and, as far as I know, we're just not capable of making this kind of equipment yet.

James was in a bad way – I'm not sure how he kept going in our earlier shoot-out. It sounds like he had a tough time; the MedLab staff have managed to ascertain that he was questioned and beaten up by the bunker staff. He has cuts, bruises, some broken ribs, two broken fingers, and shattered bones in one foot. Nothing that MedLab can't fix with their tech, even though he'll still be sore for some time.

It turns out that he and Mum knew each other years ago. Mum was in the military for a short time. She never told us that! We all have a lot of catching up to do when all of this is over – if it ends happily of course.

It turns out, and we all concur, that Nat and I are central to whatever is going on. We are linked up to the events in the bunkers, but nobody can figure out how. We all agree that it seems to be DNA based.

Nat and I together could operate the Transporters. We're trying not to call them lifts any more, not now we know what they can do, but they still look and work like lifts. Very powerful lifts. Having initially activated the Transporters together, it looks like we can then operate them on our own. We're not sure of all this stuff yet, we're just piecing together what we know, and what we've seen. We're certain though that we can get to the other bunkers via the Transporters.

Magnus thinks he can figure out how to establish easy communications between the bunkers, and he's going to prioritize that.

We talk about the neck devices. So far I've seen blue, red, and now yellow. Magnus is taken by surprise at this – he genuinely seems not to have noticed. They're easy things to miss, but once you've seen them pulsating, they're much simpler to spot. He assigns a team to analyse the neck devices as a matter of urgency.

And then there's Simon who seems to remain very quiet when we're talking about the neck implants. I think he's being cagey, but he certainly seems to be on our side. There's no doubt that he saved Mum's life. He also helped get most of us safely into Quadrant 3. He's admitted that he is Global Consortium staff, and said he was on a special mission in the area and got called in at the last minute to the bunker. Magnus has accepted that, particularly as he's managed to call up his records and can see that Simon has basic access in the bunkers. But I'm not so sure.

With the exception of my family, everybody else was recruited and trained to be here. The cuckoos in the nest are Simon and the entire Tracy family. Well, at least we've made an impact.

Finally there's Doctor Pierce. Nat could barely contain herself when he came up for debate. But the consensus of opinion is – as far as bunker staff are concerned – it was Doctor Pierce who was central to the recruitment and training process, he is their only source of information relating to Global Consortium plans and, for now at least, they must keep communications open with him. He is the common thread that links us all.

Nat is obviously put out about this, but she seems unwilling to tell us why. I'm getting a very acute sense of strong emotions there, but she's not ready to share this information yet.

So, that's where we are right now. And we have a plan. Mum isn't happy, but she's going to have to accept that Nat and I are up to our necks in this whether we all like it or not. Your main players have to step onto the battlefield. And, as unlikely as it sounds, it appears that Nat and I are the key players. Nobody is going anywhere without our help.

So here's the plan. The drones are being launched from Quadrant 1. Kate doesn't have access to the lower levels. Nat and I have not seen the drones yet, so I reckon that they must be in the area of Level 4 that I didn't get to explore yet. We were distracted by the Transportation Area at the time.

We're going to give Simon and Mum access to Level 3 so that they can take a look around at some of that weaponry. Magnus is going to try and make contact with the other two bunkers – it's important to establish a communication flow between the underground locations that Kate has not yet accessed.

We have the Comms-Tabs, we have some weapons now and we're going to take some of Magnus's security team to guard each entrance of the lift – the Transporter – while we're all creeping around in Quadrant 1.

That's the plan. Stop the drones, make contact with the other Quadrants, figure out what Kate is up to and how to stop her. Seems fair enough to me. Nothing moves forward without stopping the drones.

As if on cue, there is a distant, deep boom and a strong, persistent vibration rumbles through the bunker. The alert sirens sound in our meeting room and throughout the rest of the facility. The drones have begun to arrive at their destination, the first missile has found its target.

'They're here,' says Magnus, standing up. 'You all know what you have to do.

'We'll be able to withstand this for a short time, but if they get a direct hit on the main grid nodes, we'll start to struggle.

'Without a direct hit, I reckon we'll have a few hours maximum before we start to see structural damage, it just depends how powerful those things are.

'Let's move!' he says urgently.

As we get up from our seats, the doors to the Meeting Room slide open. It's Dad and James. Dad is his normal self again, I see it immediately. James looks amazing, considering the state he was in only half an hour ago. It's time I changed my doctor.

They're here because they want to be involved in whatever's going to happen next. James teams up with Mum, I guess that makes sense. These two have a back history.

I see a look on Dad's face like he senses something that he wasn't a part of. He parks it for now, he knows that, for the time being at least, this is all about business. Simon says he'll work alone, but go to Level 3 with Mum and James.

Then Dad surprises us all. 'I can help here,' he says. 'I know how to get access to The Global Consortium mainframe.'

23:01 Quadrant 4: Dixia Cheng, Beijing

Xiang had drawn a blank. She'd explored the entire bunker but could not figure out how to reach the storage unit for the embryos. It would be quite a sizeable area and it would need to be kept very cold.

The only suggestion that she could find to indicate that there might be some other area beyond the main bunker was in the lift. She'd noticed it earlier when they'd first gathered at the facility, prior to the darkness falling: two unusual markings on the lift. She pressed the buttons, nothing. She pressed them in different combinations, but still nothing. She knew that the key lay in those unusual buttons, but she didn't have the required access. If only she knew where this lift went – there had to be some hidden areas in this bunker.

Resigned for now, and alerted by a message from the Control Room, Xiang headed back to her position of command. Data was showing that the first drones had reached their target in the USA. She calculated that they probably had thirty minutes to an hour before the strikes began on her own facility, before the lives of her own team were put at risk, but more importantly, before the onslaught began which could end in the destruction of millions of embryos.

Earth's second chance.

Chapter Two

Exposed

Mike had never been to the Head Teacher's office before, and certainly not because of any misdemeanours, so he wasn't quite sure what to expect. He was met by two women and one man, all wearing dark suits: dark suits which meant business. They all wore ID tags, each one showing the same Global Consortium logo that had appeared on his computer screen only hours earlier.

They dismissed the Head Teacher from his own office. He went too. Clearly his authority didn't extend to these people. The bottom line was that Mike was in big trouble. They were confiscating his computer equipment. He was to cease all hacking operations immediately.

If he agreed to accept these terms without fuss, his parents would not find out that he had been stealing bandwidth from his father's employer. They would make up the financial discrepancy, alter the data records, and erase any history of Mike's activities.

If he didn't accept the terms, he would be revealed as a thief. His father would lose his job for misuse of company equipment. It would not play out well.

Mike was only young, but he knew when he'd been caught red-handed. He had no choice but to agree. By the time he got home, his computer rig was gone. His secret hook up with his dad's ISDN line had been removed. There was no evidence that he'd ever even carried out any computing in that room.

Later, when his parents asked about what had happened, he'd simply announced that he was tired of computing and that he wanted more fresh air. Now that would be the day.

Nobody knew what happened to Mike that day. The school was not told what was going on, neither were Mike's parents. The three dark-suited visitors had given him the lowdown on what The Computer

Misuse Act meant, and having just turned sixteen, there was no getting away with its penalties. Mike was well and truly warned off and terrified to return to The Global Consortium site – for the time being at least.

Because they'd missed something crucial when they'd removed the equipment from his bedroom. Concealed underneath his copy of 'The Hacker's Handbook' 1989 edition was the dot matrix printout that he'd made alongside his homework. It was the code matrix to access the wormhole that he'd created earlier, the wormhole that would remain open and undetected for many years before he would have the need to access it once again.

23:03 Quadrant 2: Balaklava Bay, Crimea

Viktor knew very well how to prioritize in times of extreme stress and pressure. As he watched the dots on his screen which represented the sixty or more drones heading towards his own bunker, he understood that they probably had about twenty to forty minutes before the strikes began.

The bunker was buried deep below the ground, surrounded by solid rock, so it would take some continued bombardment to inflict fatal damage. This facility was capable of surviving a direct nuclear strike of up to 100 kilotons. But even hidden beneath 120 metres of thick rock, that end would certainly come. There were so many drones launched that any other outcome was unthinkable.

For Viktor, rather than panic or issue ridiculous orders, this was the time for calm reflection, a chance to look at the angles and assess the possibilities. His increased Tier 10 security access had revealed the true purpose of his own Quadrant. It was two-fold. Quadrant 2 was essentially a place of growth and renewal.

Somewhere – deeper below the ground – Viktor's own research had been deployed for human benefit, to grow crops hundreds of metres beneath the Earth's surface, in darkness and using tidal seawater.

But this bunker had a much more sinister and destructive purpose too. He'd not been unduly surprised as he read the briefing notes. Quadrant 1 was not the only bunker that was armed. Viktor's bunker was ideally positioned to access the Black Sea. Previously it had been used as an underground submarine base during the Cold War. It had been selected by The Global Consortium for precisely that reason.

Now it could be used to launch drone submarines. Over two hundred of them were concealed in this place. Only Viktor was unable to access them. They lay somewhere beyond his access level, hidden for a time and enemy unknown.

The truth is that they were never supposed to be needed as part of the Genesis 2 project. But like all good strategists, some clever person deep within The Global Consortium had deemed it essential to maintain a defensive capability, or even an offensive one if that's how things played out. Just like the drones in Quadrant 1, Viktor's bunker was capable of unleashing massive firepower, concealed by the waters of the Black Sea.

Viktor now had two objectives: to make contact with the other two bunkers which had not yet been taken over by whoever it was who had sabotaged this project. And, if that failed, to find a way to launch his vast underwater armoury, to annihilate the opposition and preserve the lives of his own countrymen.

23:11 Quadrant 1: Troywood, Fife

The doors open to Level 3 and Mum, Simon and James get out, accompanied by three of the security guards who will wait by this exit. I'm relieved to see that Kate is not there waiting for us, she still only has control of the top two levels. For now.

Mum hugs Nat and me and looks at us in a 'they're growing up fast, aren't they?' kind of way. I've grown up faster in the past two days than I have at any other time in my life, even I recognize that fact.

One thing that we did all agree on in the Meeting Room earlier is that we'll only use stun devices, not proper weaponry. There's a strong feeling here that Kate and her team are not doing this of their own volition. There's no desire to cause any more deaths than are necessary. So Magnus has issued us with devices that can kill, but which are set to stun. I'm not quite ready for that level of aggression yet – I may be naive, but I've no desire to hurt anybody. I saw the state of James earlier, that's quite enough rough stuff for me. I'll be getting everybody together for a group hug at this rate.

So Mum, Simon and James set off to check out Level 3, and Nat and I head down to Level 4 with our own security team. We get six officers from the Quadrant 3 security team. Maybe they don't trust us, we're allocated twice as many guards. We're all linked by Comms-Tabs and we're in constant contact with Dad.

I just learned something else about my parents in the last ten minutes. Apparently Dad was a bit of a hacker when he was a teenager, in the days when computers were powered by petrol and screens had slightly more definition than an Etch-A-Sketch.

Magnus has given him access to one of the terminals in the Control Room – and the assistance of some of his best tech people. Dad reckons he has something which might be useful. I don't want to be negative about my dad, but I do wonder what he might have that could help us here. An online video of a piano playing cat perhaps?

Nat and I walk along the corridor of Level 4 – it's still eerily quiet down here. We pass the Transportation Area, but it's the double doors right at the far end of this curving corridor that Nat and I want to get a look at. It seems to take us ages to get there, we must be really deep underground.

Nat and I are key to all of this of course. We need to stay alert because the team on Level 3 are going nowhere without Nat and me to operate the Transporter. I place my hand on the panel which operates these doors and they slide open. Nat and I are stunned at the sheer size of this area. It's absolutely vast. I'm no sporting expert, but I would estimate that it's the size of twenty or so football pitches. Like bats in a cave, there are hundreds of drones filling this massive area.

As if activated remotely by some dark force, one by one the drones light up, two red lights like the eyes of a devil. It looks to me like most of this hangar is still full. I'd guess around a quarter of the drones have been launched so far. I would estimate there to be five hundred or more of the things still in here. How many must have been launched already and what kind of firepower do they carry? I shudder just thinking about it.

These evil devices are what are currently bombarding the Quadrant in the US. It seems eerie to watch them launching here, knowing where they are heading. It's a good job they can't travel as fast as we can in the Transporters: they still have to use airborne technology to fly over to their destinations.

There's a rumble at the far side of the hangar. Nat and I are shocked at first, but we quickly realize what is happening. A vast door is opening onto the darkness beyond, but it is shielded by a wonderful blanket array of lights which I can only assume stands between this atmosphere and whatever it is that is lurking outside. Effectively, somebody just wound down a window, but fortunately it's not letting any air in from outside.

Whatever is out there looks more blue than black to me, although it may be this protective field that is causing that effect. The drones in this sector of the hangar activate one at a time, and as they do so they rise about one metre in the air, hover there as if waiting their turn, then shoot off at some speed beyond the bunker, towards their destinations. Just like wasps leaving the nest. And with the same spiteful intent, no doubt.

I'm taking all of this in, but Nat is ahead of me. We're here to find out how to stop these things. There's nobody in this massive hangar area, just us and the drones. But Nat has found a control panel area – it looks small and insignificant in this vast, open aerodrome.

However deep underground we are, this area

seems to open to the outside world; we must be buried in a hill or mountain. I wasn't particularly aware of the terrain when we entered as tourists. At that time I thought I was on a pleasant family day out. I hadn't been expecting to save the world.

Nat is studying the console. It's made up of the usual high-tech, multiple screens, no visible power supply and, of course, no instruction leaflet. Why anybody thought that we could sort this out I don't know. Nat is combing the area like she's part of a police forensics team when I rest my hand on a circular panel in the work area. It's like a built-in mouse mat, but it doesn't have a picture of a cartoon character on it like the one I use at home.

A small, technical unit disengages from underneath the screen on my right and the console powers down. Just like that. 'You're kidding?' I say to Nat. The drones that were in the process of activation stop dead, like somebody just switched off the fridge.

The vast doors all around the hangar, not just the one that opened a few minutes previously, all close slowly and heavily and as the thud of metal on metal is heard, the force field protecting us from whatever is outside also disappears.

The hangar is still. The drones have stopped. I call Magnus on the Comms-Tab.

'Have they stopped, Magnus?' I ask, not quite believing that it can be as simple as this.

After a few moments Magnus replies. He's just consulted with the Quadrant 3 Control Room. 'The drones in the air are still activated,' he says, 'but we can see that they are no longer leaving the bunker.'

'Good work Dan!' says Magnus, 'Did you get the enabling unit?'

I assume he means the bit that just popped out a moment or two ago, so I pick it up and answer 'Yes'.

'Bring it with you!' replies Magnus. 'Come and join us back here in Quadrant 3 as soon as you can.'

I pick up the enabling unit and grin at Nat. 'Mission accomplished!' I say, feeling pleased with myself. Moments ago this area was launching powerful weapons intent on destroying the remaining three bunkers. There are still scores of drones up in the air, but at least we held back the tide.

'Don't be so sure Dan,' cautions Nat. 'I know these people and they're clever – and ruthless.'

There it is again. She knows something and she's holding it back.

We stroll towards the double doors and press the button to exit, stepping out into the long corridor. Although it's a long way up to the top, and the curve is obscuring our view, we can just see enough from here to know that Kate must have got access to this area.

The six people guarding the Transporter door on our behalf are lying on the floor, unconscious or dead, we can't see from this distance. And the people who shot them are now heading in our direction, weapons at the ready and trained directly on us.

Enabled

Kate had received her briefing from Doctor Pierce and was to await the final codes, which he anticipated would be available shortly. Her new Tier 20 security access now put at her fingertips the full truth about the hidden levels below and their sinister secrets: secrets which were to have remained concealed, extreme contingency planning only for the Genesis 2 project.

She'd barely had time to digest the full extent of that information when Doctor Pierce re-established contact to provide the final piece of information that she needed. The kids had taken the bait. In fact they'd all fallen for it, Magnus as well. He'd certainly chosen the right Custodian to lead this sabotage. Kate had already shown herself to be ruthlessly focused and efficient.

When the boy had placed his hand on the activation pad, in that very instant he'd had his DNA signature harvested remotely. The sequencer had taken it, analysed it, re-created the patterns and duplicated it. Doctor Pierce had digitally replicated Dan's DNA. Kate and her team could now access any of the areas that had been pre-activated by the twins. If only they'd got the girl's DNA too, that would have opened up all four Quadrants immediately.

But for now, they'd just gained access to the lower levels of Quadrant 1. Wherever the twins went, Kate would follow. Quadrant 3 was next. But that would first require Kate to access her bunker's darkest secret deep down on the lower levels.

Chapter Three

Access

Mike tapped at the virtual keypad which was projected just in front of him in the Control Room. Although he knew more than a thing or two about computers, he still preferred to use keyboards rather than motion swipes to control his tech. Some old habits die hard.

It took him a few moments to acclimatize himself to the device, which was the fastest bit of kit he'd ever used. They appeared to have much more than superfast broadband in this bunker. 'Typical Government,' Mike thought to himself, 'Keeping the fastest broadband to themselves!'

He couldn't figure out who made this terminal – there was no logo or brand name that he recognized – but he resolved to check the store catalogue when he got back home to see if he could buy one. He suspected though that this would not be available in the shops.

After taking a few moments to get over his initial disorientation, Mike figured out where everything was that he needed to use and set about entering the system via the wormhole, a wormhole that he'd left open twenty-three years ago. The chances of it having been undetected all this time were surely remote and, even then, who even knew if it was connected with whatever his family were caught up within the bunker?

Sometimes the human brain can make huge leaps and seemingly bizarre connections. That's what Mike had done here. Random elements of his life seemed to be fusing together: a threatening warning as a teenager; the reappearance of a child who he thought was dead; a son who seemed to have some kind of special powers, and a war that threatened the future of the planet. These things had to be connected. He didn't know how just yet, but he was very pleased that he'd left that wormhole open all those years ago.

He'd memorized the details on that old dot matrix printout, because he'd taken it out and looked at it so many times in the intervening years: never daring to hack back in to take another look, but always wondering what lay in that particular box of secrets.

Mike tapped away, occasionally seeking the assistance of the technical experts that Magnus had assigned to him. Even Mike's key tech assistant looked on in awe as she watched him work. Her look was like the one a nuclear engineer might give to a retired RAF pilot talking through the mechanics of an old jet engine. Their experiences are miles apart – and one is working with an old technology – but the knowledge, expertise and skill never go away even though the tech used might no longer be fashionable – or cool.

Mike knew his stuff, and he was soon on comfortable territory. The speed of his finger movements accelerated wildly as he could see his final destination in the distance. A code here. A password there. Enter the code matrix that he'd created all those years ago. A double click … and he was in.

A distinctive logo showed crisp and in sharp definition on the screen. It was actually in 3D. Mike stopped short of embarrassing himself by reaching out to try to touch the logo. There were younger eyes on him and he didn't want to appear to be too much of a 'dad'.

A small group had gathered around Mike's terminal, sensing that something important and impressive was going on. The distinctive logo rotated slowly in the desk space just in front on Mike. It was proof of his success. His wormhole had stood the test of time. His coding skills as a teenager had sat there undetected for over twenty years. They were in.

Mike had full access to The Global Consortium

systems. He had the Genesis 2 project at his fingertips.

23:17 Quadrant 3: White Sulphur Springs, West Virginia

Magnus sat at a remote secured terminal in the Quadrant 3 Meeting Room. The blinds were shut, but he'd brought in a young comms engineer called Sam to assist him.

Like Mike, Magnus was what you might call a highly accomplished geek. He'd had a similar background to the other Custodians, which was why he now found himself in this particular role.

Magnus had been a tech entrepreneur in his former life, the head of Magnum Enterprises. He'd created the world's first adaptive algorithm. In short, it was just a few steps away from allowing tech to think and adapt according to circumstances.

The applications of his discovery had been immediately enormous, yet threatening. Like Mike, he'd received a visit from a group of officials in suits. Unlike Mike they'd come to court him, not to intimidate him to stop his activities.

Magnus was given a very substantial amount of money not to make the algorithm commercially available. In fact, as far as the tech world was concerned, he was a geek 'has been'. The great discovery which had been promised on the cover of Time Magazine had never really come to anything and Magnus had disappeared from the spotlight.

Most people never thought about him again. Others assumed he'd overpromised and under-delivered and been cast aside. In actual fact, he had millions of dollars in the bank and a custom built office suite – along with the best tech minds in the world – working on some top secret projects in Detroit. Hidden in open view.

While the rest of the world mourned an economy gone bad, Magnus worked on projects which could have paid for every person in that state to own their own palace – if his work was ever released commercially that is. But this work was never going to see the light of day, not in an industrial setting at least.

An adaptive algorithm was the biggest breakthrough in tech that only a handful of people were ever going to know about. Using this algorithm, computers and laptops could self-diagnose, learn and adapt from problems and expand their memory exponentially. It meant that computer-powered cars could effectively heal themselves by diagnosing problems and making ongoing adjustments, regenerating themselves as new and improved models, and actually 'learning' with every mile that was travelled.

Magnus had created the algorithm that would eventually make computers sentient. It could not make them feel, but it gave them – in tech terms – the same ability to learn, reflect, consider, weigh up, and improve that the human brain experiences.

Concealed below ground under the ruins of an abandoned factory, if anybody had cared to notice, they'd have seen some of the most expensive cars imaginable driving in and out of the vandalized entrance to an underground car park. Where they went, nobody would have known. Like bees, they entered and left, one, sometimes two, at a time. What honey they were making, nobody knew.

Magnus had become an expert at war games in his secret, underground offices. Among many other applications that his teams had discovered for his algorithm, they'd come up with a military deployment that had made somebody at the top of the command chain very excited.

Magnus had created it originally as a device to assist people with disabilities, whose bodies lay out of their control, even though their minds might still be sharp and alert. He'd been inspired – and moved – by the case of people with 'locked-in syndrome', a terrible condition where patients cannot move or communicate verbally due to complete paralysis of virtually all of their voluntary muscles, with the exception of the eyes.

Magnus had created an exoskeleton using his algorithm. This amazing device would allow people with locked-in syndrome to move once again. The adaptive algorithm could learn what the test subject wanted to do at an incredible speed and – as it adapted faster and faster – the time between eye movement and action became as instantaneous as if there were zero paralysis.

The tech teams had then begun to develop the exoskeleton as a biological component. It was effectively a layer of skin created in the lab which contained the exoskeleton in an undetectable form, like a powered suit that nobody could even see. Things then took a sudden and unfortunate turn for Magnus. Whoever was funding these projects wanted the human applications of his work to stop.

For a while Magnus had seen a glimpse of a future where people in wheelchairs could walk again and where those with Parkinson's disease would no longer suffer from the effects of tremors or stiffness. For a brief time he thought that he was going to be able to change the world, to make a remarkable difference to thousands of lives. Magnus had grown tired of his wealth, and disillusioned with his work in this underground office.

He'd experienced a spark of light when he realized how his algorithm discoveries could be used, but his employers were more interested in the military applications. Magnus had been instructed to mass produce the original, metallic exoskeletons on an industrial scale, but he didn't know what for. They wouldn't tell him. He felt as though he'd sold his soul.

The exoskeletons were to be created to a specific size and design. The biological element was not required, the strong, metallic frames of the prototypes were sufficient. He didn't know how these were going to be used, but he had an uncomfortable feeling that it would not be benefitting humanity in the way that he would have preferred.

These uncomfortable memories skimmed through his mind as Magnus considered the chain of events that had led to him being where he was right now. At last, there was a chance for him to do something meaningful. He felt as if he'd supped with the Devil during his former life in Detroit, but now, with these people, in this bunker, he hoped that he could do something that would finally help humanity.

Magnus and Sam swiftly created a scanning program which could detect and unscramble the encrypted SOS messages currently being transmitted by Viktor and Xiang, as well as from his own bunker. It was fairly simple to do, when you knew that the messages were being broadcast in the first place.

First they found their own message and backward engineered the encryption and transmission that was being sent out from their own bunker. That gave them the information that they needed to scan for the alerts being broadcast by Viktor and Xiang, because they were no longer looking for a needle in a haystack.

Once they'd found the encrypted broadcasts, Sam ran it through a clever extraction program that he'd created rapidly at his terminal. Between them, within fifteen minutes, they'd managed to locate the precise source of Viktor and Xiang's emergency broadcasts, figure out the systems and protocols used, and re-engineer it for broadcast and reception.

Magnus felt pleased with himself. This work was nourishing his soul, more than giving away many of his millions to charities and good causes could ever have done. Magnus was a man who needed to do good things. When he did things that were not so good, as he had been doing in Detroit for many years now, it sucked the life and energy out of him.

As he prepared to send the first two-way communication between Quadrants 2 and 4, Magnus finally realized that his purpose in life was to use his skills and aptitude only for good. It wasn't about money, cars and prestige for him – he just wanted to do amazing things for humanity, that's what he needed to do, it's why he was put on this Earth.

That's why it would have destroyed him to know that at that very moment, thousands of kilometres away, the exoskeletons that could have helped so many thousands of human beings were about to be deployed in a way that could potentially kill every single one of them.

23:19 Quadrant 1: Troywood, Fife

Kate has found her way to the lower levels. I hoped we'd have more time, at least to stop the drones, but she beat us to it. We've stopped the remaining drones launching at least and I'm assuming that Magnus wants that enabling unit to prevent them from being reactivated. The big question is, if only Nat and I can get down here, and we didn't set off the drones, who did? And what access do they have to this bunker?

Too many questions to answer right now. The security team is making its way along the long corridor in our direction. They're shooting, but they're not trying to hit us, they don't seem to want us dead. They want to back us into the drones' hangar, where they think they can contain us, I think.

But Nat has a plan. She'd spotted something earlier among the drones and she thinks we have a way out. As for Mum, James and Simon, they'll have to fend for themselves. I'm going to give them a tip off though – Kate may have security teams on their level by now.

I use the Comms-Tab to alert Mum and I'm relieved to hear that they're okay at the moment, even though something seems to be going on in the corridor outside. They prepare to hide, to buy themselves more time.

I contact Magnus, seeing what Nat is leading me towards now. 'Magnus, we're going to try and get to one of the other Quadrants,' I say. 'Can you communicate with them yet?'

'I'm just on it,' says Magnus. He sounds pleased

with himself.

'We're going to try for Quadrant 4, can you tell them we're coming?'

'Will do,' replies Magnus. 'Good luck!'

I hope that Kate doesn't have Comms-Tab access yet. They've only just got access to the lower levels, so I reckon that we still have a bit more time where we can communicate with each other securely.

Nat has seen a Transporter unit, much like the one we used earlier when we were first reunited. They seem to have these things all over the place down here. Nat thinks we can use this to make our escape, but unlike the lift, it's not quite so clear how these things work. Still, we don't have that many options at this moment, so I agree with Nat – we have to try. If they reach us now, with the enabling device, not only can they launch the remaining drones, they could also force Nat and me to give them access to the other Quadrants. If they don't have it already, that is.

Nat and I step on the Transporter – it seems to be here primarily to transport things rather than people. We both scan the control panel, desperately trying to remember what we did before. There's a main, larger panel, we place our hand on that. The Transporter gives a jolt, just like the lift had done earlier, as if it had recognized us in some way. Unlike the lifts, there are no numbers on this fascia, we just have to take pot luck and try and guess which of the weird symbols will take us to Quadrant 4, based on the order that they're in.

The doors slide open and the security teams are here. The hangar is vast, so it takes them a moment or two to scan the area and focus on where we are. They start to run in our direction, and Nat and I look at each other, knowing the urgency of this situation. 'That one!' we say simultaneously, pointing to the same symbol.

We press the button and the Transporter beams surge into life. The approaching security guards stop dead as they fade out of our view and our new location materializes in front of our eyes.

Chapter Four

23:20 Quadrant 4: Dixia Cheng, Beijing

Xiang was sitting at her console, wondering what could be done to avert this imminent attack. She was feeling rather useless, her bunker seemed to have no defensive capabilities. The most that she could hope for would be to preserve the lives of her team and to protect the structure of the bunker as best they could. She had her tech teams working on communicating with the other bunkers, but they had no way – it seemed – of getting in touch. Only hours ago she'd thought they were the only bunker.

Her thoughts were interrupted by a persistent alert on her E-Pad. It was an incoming message. Xiang's spirits lifted as realized what this must be. One of the other bunkers had worked out how to make a direct communication. Xiang opened up the channel and a face appeared on her E-Pad. It was an American man, middle-aged, very well groomed.

'I'm Magnus!' he exclaimed. 'I'm hoping that you're the Custodian for Quadrant 4?'

'Xiang. Pleased to meet you!' she replied. The common language in the bunkers was English. Xiang spoke five languages, but at least The Global

Consortium had thought to ensure a common language as standard protocol.

'Sending some data directly to you, unencrypt using code ZZ5llb581P,' continued Magnus, and Xiang watched as the data arrived.

Magnus was sending her updates on everything they knew and the comms information required for the three remaining Quadrants to communicate with each other. Magnus knew that he was taking a bit of a chance on this. As far as they all knew, Quadrant 1 was the only bunker that had been sabotaged, but he'd built in a remote scramble code line in the data. If Xiang proved to be hostile, he could remotely delete the data that he'd just sent her. Magnus had learned early in his career – always keep control of the 'off' button.

Xiang scanned the data quickly, passing on key elements to senior members of her team in a movement of her finger.

'You may have two people entering your bunker Xiang,' Magnus began, when he decided that she'd had enough time to get the gist of the information.

'These two young people are crucial to our ongoing safety and you need to give them everything that they ask for.

'I'm not sure where they'll surface in the bunker – in fact they're not quite sure if they'll even get to your Quadrant.

'Please read the briefing I just sent you and see what you can do to help. I'm going to establish contact with Quadrant 2 and you should do the same as soon as you can.'

Xiang was already onto it. She'd alerted her security teams, and at that very moment they were making their way to the lift areas where the two new arrivals would need to surface to access the upper bunker.

She hadn't realized how tense her breathing had been. Now there seemed to be a fighting chance: if the remaining three Quadrants could work together, there was still hope. Her fears returned instantly as the entire bunker shook as if it had been stepped on by a massive giant. The first drone had reached Beijing. The attack had begun.

23:21 Quadrant 2: Balaklava Bay, Crimea

Viktor's years spent fighting as a rebel had taught him many important things. One of those things was that sometimes you have to choose the person that you are going to be in times of battle. He was much happier immersed in nature, in his own company, away from the rest of the world. But to survive in life he'd had to become ruthless, violent and scheming. This was not his true self. He soon learned that if he was going to get through life, he'd had to make whatever changes were necessary. So he knew now what he needed to do to continue to survive.

When Magnus made contact with him via his E-Pad, he was of course relieved that the remaining three bunkers could now work together to defend themselves against the drone attack and combine their energies to defeat Quadrant 1. But as Viktor received the same data and intelligence that Xiang had read only minutes before, from an American who appeared assured and over confident, he knew what he must do to maintain the upper hand. Only he would know for now about the drone submarines that were concealed within this base. This was his trump card, his ability to turn things to his favour if force or threat became a necessity.

And now he knew from Magnus's briefing how he would access that fire power. The secret was the twins. They were the key to his plan.

Cryogenics

These Transporters are a bit like playing Russian roulette for Nat and me at the moment. We have escaped from the drone hangar, but because we can't figure out the symbols yet, we haven't a clue where we are. What we can now see though is that these Transporters work the much same as the lifts. We can move between rooms – and hopefully Quadrants – using them.

They seem to operate on the same principal as the lift too. Activation appears to need both of us, after that it looks like we can use them on our own. Whoever thought this all out must have had a strategy, but whatever it was, I can't work it out.

Still, it appears that Kate can't reach us; she doesn't seem to have what she needs to operate these Transporters. Though she now has access to the lower levels of Quadrant 1, we need to know how she did that. If she can travel as freely as we can, the remaining Quadrants are in big trouble.

Nat and I look around our new location. On the surface, it has barely changed. It's a massive hangar – more like a storage facility here though.

We are surrounded by a labyrinth of circular units of all shapes and sizes. They look like they're running at extremely low temperatures – I'd hazard a guess that we're now in a room full of refrigerators, but it's not immediately obvious what is inside them.

It's around the edges of this storage facility where the answers seem to lie though. There are thousands of pod units, clearly from the same origins as those used in the BioFiltration Area. Only these are not incubating living, breathing organisms. These have a completely different use.

Nat and I step closer. It's hard to see what's inside because of the ice and the frost in here. We rub away at the misted glass and are shocked to see the contents of these pods. They contain babies, children, teenagers, and adults. Males and females of every age up to about thirty I'd guess. Still, frozen, inanimate. Thousands of them.

We move through the pods, stunned at their contents. There are animals too: calves, cows, bulls; lambs, ewes, rams. This is an ark.

I'll bet that the cylindrical units contain embryos, I've seen how it's done on TV. This vast hangar houses thousands of humans and livestock, all frozen and awaiting their reawakening. Were they ever alive even? Maybe they have been grown entirely from embryos.

We get a message via the Comms-Tab. It's Magnus and I find his presence timely and reassuring. 'You both okay?' he asks.

'Fine,' I say, 'we seem to have transported to another Quadrant.'

'Touch the dial on your Tab, bottom right,' says Magnus.

My tab shows video, and I can see Magnus on the screen, rather than just hear him now.

'Look at this!' I say, and hold my hand up so that

he can take in the view of the hangar.

Nat does the same – we're giving him a live video show here. I can see that he's taken aback. Nothing that we ever learn about these bunkers seems to be good news.

Doctor Pierce said we were guardians of the planet. All the evidence suggests that there is something a bit more sinister going on here.

'Guys, you need to make your way to the upper levels,' Magnus continues. 'Your contacts are Xiang Liú and Viktor Gorbunov. They're both expecting you and they'll make you very welcome.

'Don't get distracted by the lower levels, our first priority must be to stop the drone attack. We must work out how to disarm or disable those airborne drones. We can work out the other stuff later!'

Magnus makes a good point – we have to try and stay on task. Mum, James and Simon could be in trouble right now, and Nat and I have to try and avoid distractions. It's like we've both been set free in a sweet shop, there are so many things to draw our attention.

'This way then!' says Nat, and we head towards the door.

The basic layout of these bunkers seems standard. They appear to have been built to the same core design, though the interiors are different depending on what they're using the space for. It's making life easier for us though. Because we're getting the hang of the layout, we know roughly which direction to head in and where the lifts should be in this place.

We step out into the long, curved corridor which mirrors the one in Quadrant 1 where only minutes earlier we were being chased by Kate's guards. The lift is the same as those in Quadrants 1 and 3, and we're relieved when it activates correctly and we press the button for Level 2, which is where the Control Room should be.

We give each other a smile when the doors slide open and we're greeted by a lady who is surrounded by security guards. It's not Kate though, this must be Xiang. She smiles and we can see that Magnus is right, they're expecting us and we're welcome here. That makes a change.

Which Quadrant though? I wish we could figure out these symbols on the Transporters. The lifts are straightforward, they're placed in order, but the Transporters are not so easy. It's like having to get to your destination using a crazy sat nav system. Actually, forget the 'crazy' bit. It's like using a regular sat nav system – you haven't got a clue where you'll end up.

We're about to step out of the lift when my Comms-Tab comes alive. It's Mum, audio only. She's whispering, 'We're in big trouble here guys, you should see what's down here.'

23:59 Quadrant 1: Troywood, Fife

Kate descended to the third level in the lift. Only minutes earlier it had been blocked to her, but now they had digitally replicated Dan's DNA signature they had full access to the lower levels.

She had been momentarily annoyed when the security team had informed her that the twins had escaped from the drones' area via one of the Transporters. No problem, the youngster had activated it and that's all she needed. With the DNA signature field currently glowing over the surface of her hand like an electronic glove, she knew now that anywhere Dan went, she could follow.

Assisted by the guidance of Doctor Pierce, they'd created an electronic glove – a SymNode – which enabled Kate and her team to cheat the Transporters into thinking that they were being operated by Dan.

It mattered very little that the drone launches had been stopped – there were enough of them in the air to destroy all three Quadrants. It would take a little time, but eventually they'd break and crumble. Besides, she would soon have control of all four Quadrants anyway now she had access to this bunker's lower levels. She would be able to access her bunker's darkest secret.

Earlier, Dan had caught a glimpse of the military equipment and uniforms in this area, and taken a few moments to wonder why it was there, and who it was for. Kate knew the answer to this question. In fact it was the very reason that she was travelling to this level right now.

Before they pursued and caught the twins, she needed to gain the upper hand. To do that she would have to unleash Quadrant 1's full military capacity. As she commanded her security team, Kate was unaware that she was being watched by Amy, James and Simon who had concealed themselves hastily when Dan had alerted them to the impending intrusion.

Amy whispered quietly via her Comms-Tab as Magnus, Dan and Nat hung on to her every word in Quadrants 3 and 4. 'Press the dial, bottom right on your tab,' said Nat. 'It gives a video feed.'

Xiang joined Nat and Dan as they all watched Kate as she first touched a panel on the wall, revealing a hidden entrance. She looked like she was wearing an electronic glove, her hand seemed to be surrounded by some sort of electronic field.

The doors slid open, and the units concealed within the room activated. They could make out movement, Amy's hand began shaking and it took a few moments until everybody could see exactly what was stepping out of this room. One by one they came. With heavy, purposeful, threatening movements. Part human and part machine. And definitely built for war. They watched in fear as Kate's new cyborg army lined up, ready for inspection.

They were getting ready for the final assault.

Chapter Five

Concealed

One thing that a sociopath is adept at doing is hiding those terrible traits. And so, after the visit to the psychologist, things seemed to calm down and the parents wondered if it had been a 'phase', perhaps just a bad and very extended case of the 'terrible twos'.

After a few months they dared to hope that both of their adopted children might – after all – be okay. Which parent ever wants to think that their child might be ill in some way, especially if that would lead to them being abhorred or detested by the rest of society?

The child was learning fast. Although consumed with evil and hateful thoughts, the best way to be able to continue with spiteful manipulations is to do it undetected. When nobody knows what you're doing, you can just get on with it, unhindered by interference. So the child learned to adapt.

The future killer is best concealed, in open view, where they are accepted and integrated. The child learned skills of charm, engagement and likability, but the hate that festered deep inside never went away. It was just waiting, incubating, biding its time – until it would be unleashed, unfettered and destructive.

So when an accident happened at school, or something got lost, broken or stolen, the child was nowhere to be seen. There was never any evidence, no trail left behind, nobody who could point an accusing finger and present any proof of involvement. Yet everywhere the child went, a trail of destruction followed.

Nobody really noticed the pattern, and the parents – who might have had a slight inkling of what was going on – just denied it to themselves, relieved that they were no longer having to consult the psychologist. But this evil child was bound to a sibling in a very special way. A biological tie that was more than just flesh and blood.

They weren't just members of the same family. They were twins.

00:12 Quadrant 3: White Sulphur Springs, West Virginia

Mike had actually got a spontaneous round of applause as he'd broken into The Global Consortium files. He hadn't realized as he'd been typing away that such a crowd had gathered. But there was a ripple of excitement running through the Control Room, a sensation that something rather spectacular was going on here.

Like Amy and her military career, Mike's aptitude with tech had gone largely unnoticed by his kids. The stuff they shared – the funny web videos, the endless picture memes and the occasional animated GIF – that was for family. But before Mike had left his work to stay at home with Dan, he'd worked in tech, and continued to channel his inner hacker on more 'above board' projects.

The language used to describe a day job can be so deceptive. When Mike was asked what he did as a profession, he'd just brush the question aside with a joke, saying that he was 'an IT guy' or a 'salaried geek'. People would laugh and think nothing of it. To his kids and family, he just seemed to spend a lot of time tapping on his keyboard. Doing ... who knows what?

When Mike was on a PC or laptop, it was like an elite athlete getting ready to race in the Olympics. Only in Mike's case, there were no muscles and the athletic body was just an aspiration. But his sport was tech and at this he excelled.

So it would only be a matter of time before he started to unlock some of the secrets that had been so well hidden by The Global Consortium.

00:32 Quadrant 4: Dixia Cheng, Beijing

It's very disconcerting sitting in this bunker with explosions rocking the entire structure every few minutes

'How well protected are we down here?' Nat had asked, voicing the fears that all of us were thinking.

Xiang had a structural expert explain it to us in words that we understood. These bunkers can survive a nuclear attack, but not direct hits. The drones are not armed with nukes, so at least that's good news. However, they are highly explosive and have the capacity to do critical damage to the bunkers. Any direct hits in key locations could cause a number of problems for us. Air filtration systems can be damaged, power supplies cut or structural damage done.

More worrying for Xiang is the fact that her bunker lies beneath the structures of the city. Every time a drone strikes, it will be damaging the buildings above, killing and injuring defenceless people as they lie oblivious in the stasis brought about by the darkness outside. We really need to stop these drones.

We've had twenty minutes or so to be briefed by Xiang and her team, and Nat and I have shared the information about the embryos that we discovered on the floors below. Xiang is not surprised by this, her data has already indicated this to be the case – but she's very pleased that Nat and I can give her and her team direct access to the lower levels.

She wants to take blood, DNA and tissue samples from us. I'm put to shame by Nat who steps forward willingly. We both know that there's something special about us that we don't understand just yet, but it's not so interesting to me that I want to be poked and prodded.

'You get used to it!' says Nat, once again hinting at things that have happened that I have yet to learn about.

Fortunately, the same as everything else in these bunkers, the kit is like nothing I've ever seen before. No needles, no sight of blood and nothing cut. I'm relieved, I thought Nat was about to reveal me for the big coward that I really am. I don't mind the odd ray gun, but an injection? That's really pushing my limits.

Xiang quite obviously can't wait to get her hands on those samples – and to be completely honest, I really hope that we get some answers from her team. I want to know what's going on with Nat and me, yet I'm afraid of what I might learn. I always felt different, it's why things went so haywire for me at school. But I'm scared of what the truth might reveal to me.

Xiang assures us that we couldn't be in a better place to discover the secrets that our bodies are holding, so that's good news to be getting on with.

It's the more pressing issues that concern us though. The video feed captured by Mum's Comms-Tab cycles around on the main screen in the conference room. The enhanced graphics pick out, highlight and analyse what's going on with these cybernetic soldiers or whatever they are.

They have what appears to be a robotic spinal column, running from the base of their skull right down to their coccyx. We know that because they came out of that room in their underwear. It all looks very threatening – it's all linked to a light, metallic exoskeleton.

Presumably the military clothing and paraphernalia that I'd spotted in Quadrant 1 much earlier must be for their use. I get the impression they're going to be a lot more effective than the security teams that Kate has had to work with so far. At the top and to the side of the spinal columns is a faint black light, just like the ones Mum and Kate's people have, just below the surface of the skin and concealed in the neck.

I've been careless. I glance closely at Xiang to see

if she or her team have the neural implants fitted. They do. They are green in this Quadrant, but they do not appear to be active at the moment. I am relieved, we can trust Xiang. At least, for now. We can tell who the 'good guys' and the 'bad guys' are for the time being – the red devices are the big problem, I've a feeling though that we're looking at some really bad guys on that video feed.

Mum, Simon and James have gone undetected on Level 3 of Kate's Quadrant; they're keeping out of sight for now, trying to figure out what the plan is, looking for a way to land us an advantage in this battle. Levels 3 and 4 are unfamiliar to Kate at present, so we have a little time to regroup, and Mum and her team can remain undetected for a short time. We're most concerned about how Kate has access to those lower levels.

Apparently this is Xiang's area of expertise, but she thinks Nat and I have access to these transportation systems via our DNA. She reckons it must be connected to our genetic code in some way. Xiang says it has to be something unique and bound to each individual person. That's mind blowing to me, so I go with the flow for now.

We've handed over the enabling unit to Xiang's tech guys who scanned it and 3D printed it out for Magnus via a secure channel that the three Quadrants have now set up with Magnus's help. I can't even get a bit of paper to print out straight on our printer at home.

Finally, it seems Dad is doing some spectacular stuff at his terminal in Quadrant 3. He got a spontaneous round of applause according to Magnus. Must have shown them the video of that piano playing cat I reckon. So that's where we're up to right now.

We have assembled small pieces of information, but nobody can see the overall picture just yet. The one person that we haven't heard from for some time is Doctor Pierce. Everybody seems hell bent on working out what Nat and I have to do with all of this, but I think more of the answers lie with Doctor Pierce. Nat will have some things to say about that I'm absolutely sure.

I suggest to Xiang that we try to raise Doctor Pierce via the Operations Centre that I'm assuming will be found on her lower levels. These bunkers all seem to have the same basic layout, as if they were designed from a single blueprint. Maybe they were saving money on architect's fees. Xiang thinks that's a good idea, and Nat is also very keen to get more information about Doctor Pierce.

I touch my Comms-Tab and speak to Magnus.

'Do you think there's any way that you can trace Doctor Pierce's secure channel back from the broadcast he made to me in Quadrant 1?' I ask.

'We'll need to get your mum's team over there if we can to clone the encryption data on that terminal,' replies Magnus. 'I'll get onto her now.

'They're pretty caught up avoiding Kate down there, it may take some time.

'You should try to get to Quadrant 2 to meet Viktor if you can too,' Magnus continues. 'He's very anxious to access the lower levels of his own bunker, he thinks that he may have something that can help us.'

Viktor will need Nat and me to access the lower levels. It makes sense to me that we should give all the Quadrants full access so that we can fight these drones – and Kate – with whatever we can throw at them.

'What damage have the drones done so far?' Nat interrupts, as our own bunker shakes once again from an explosion at ground level. More of the city above in ruins. More lives lost. Who is doing this, and why?

'We expect to be on top of this thing very soon,' Magnus continues confidently. 'We need to keep an eye on what Kate is doing with her new army of Troopers, that's our next problem.'

'Xiang, can you come up with something creative at the Transporter where Nat and Dan entered your Quadrant?'

Magnus looks mischievous. 'Perhaps have some explosives ready, and plenty of armed guards concealed to greet them if they arrive.'

Magnus is right. Kate seems to be able to follow us wherever Nat and I have activated Transporters. Xiang needs to guard that area in case Kate plans to invade us with her new army of cyborgs, or whatever they are.

We decide to head to the lower levels of Xiang's Quadrant, to give her teams access to what's down there, to defend the Transporter that we used to get here, and make our way to Quadrant 2 to meet Viktor.

Everything is still in limbo, but we appear to be making progress, I feel like any time now somebody is going to make a connection and we're going to take a big leap forward.

I'm right. Magnus's voice comes up on the Comms-Tab and he's obviously in a state of high excitement.

'I've found out where to locate the code sequences,' he announces. 'We can stop the drones!'

He pauses, and we're uncertain if it's time to start celebrating the news.

'The only thing is …' he hesitates before continuing – that usually means bad news is coming.

'Dan and Nat, you're going to have to return to Quadrant 1. I need you back in the drone hangar.'

Chapter Six

Beyond The Karman Line

The satellite matrix surrounding the Earth had the appearance of a prison cell when viewed from above. It may have been that the planet inside was contained for its own protection – or it could have been that it was caught behind bars. Does the animal in the zoo think that its captors are caged and that it is free? It all depends on perception.

Docked to one of the largest satellites, outside the matrix and on the very edge of space, was a large, illuminated sphere. It had windows to look out into space – at the vast and unexplored area beyond the Earth, and down below, at the ailing planet which was currently enveloped in a blue shroud.

Right at the centre of this orb, deep within its sturdy exterior, sat a lone man. He was middle-aged, his work area was sparse and he wore an unusual tie. He was surrounded by projections of faces – there were almost two hundred of them – they were holograms.

The man seemed worried. He had a grave look on his face, and as he discussed matters with the assembled group it was obvious that he was having difficulty accounting for himself. The faces were those of the world's leaders whose physical bodies were in stasis along with the population below. They were never supposed to be woken, but this man had been forced by drastic circumstances to resort to emergency planning procedures.

He had communicated secret information to the Custodians of the three bunkers which were so far free from sabotage. He had spoken to one of the twins, the boy Dan, who didn't yet know how the future of the planet below had been placed so precariously in his hands. Now he had awoken the consciences of the world's leaders as their physical bodies slept on the Earth's surface far below him.

They were angry and in disagreement. He'd assured them once that this situation could not occur. Now they were learning that their planet might never awaken from its current sleep – and that all those years of careful planning may well have been in vain.

Concealed

Amy watched the Troopers lining up in military fashion, a formation which she recognized from years ago. At one time she could have done this, moved in perfect unison, drilled and trained for precision and discipline. Only there was something quite inhuman about these soldiers.

Kate was in charge here, and it looked as if she was ready to discard her old security team in favour of these soldiers. They were far superior physically, in height, build and strength. They were exactly the kind of army that you would want to have at your command and fighting on your side.

Amy gestured to Simon and James – all three had taken up positions where they could not be detected. They knew that they would not be able to stay hidden for long, there were too many soldiers assembling here now. They also knew that, once armed, this new army would not be such an easy pushover as the bunker security teams had been.

All three had been monitoring the Comms-Tab conversations that had been patched through to them. The devices were superb in a military situation – with no speakers there was nothing to alert Kate's guards to their presence there. There was even a silent text-to-speech option, allowing constant contact and information transfer.

There was a new plan. Amy wasn't happy about it. She'd only just been reunited with her daughter and she wasn't pleased to be exposing her once again to such extreme risk. But she knew for sure that there was really no choice. Dan and Nat were crucial to events in these bunkers and, however fearful she was, they would have to play out their role in this situation. Besides, without Dan and Nat, they were all trapped.

Magnus wanted Dan and Nat to return a rewired enabling unit to the hangar area. He also needed somebody to clone the encrypted data that Doctor Pierce had used for his secured broadcasts to Dan.

Sometimes you get a break in life. That's what happened at that moment. All of the troops had been assembled, and were now being moved along the corridor to the weaponry and uniform area. The electronic glove worn by Kate had been replicated on the hands of several more senior members of her security team – seemingly just by touch – and this appeared to be what was giving them access to all of the rooms on this lower level.

There were just three regular guards left once the troops had vacated the area. Simon, Amy and James took one each, and in no time at all three unconscious bodies were locked up in storage boxes – minus their uniforms, which were now being worn by the three imposters. All three had received military training, albeit for Simon and Amy some years ago now. But they looked authentic and nobody really took much notice of them as they headed off towards the lift and ultimately the hangar area where Nat and Dan would meet them and transport them back to safety. They needed access to the lift first though, and they'd need one of those electronic gloves to activate it.

Magnus's guards had only been shot unconscious which was a relief for Amy. They were just being escorted into the lift, presumably for interrogation. James knew what that would entail. Magnus's team was quick to catch on – they recognized Amy, James and Simon and, on their signal, when they were all in the lift, they swiftly managed to overcome the four guards who'd been assigned to escort the prisoners. One of the guards was wearing an electronic glove. Amy asked him how to transfer it to her hand and it was soon clear that he had no intention of answering that question.

Then Simon stepped forward. He armed his weapon and put his booted foot on the guard's hand, aiming his gun in the centre of it. 'You have five seconds to answer the question, then I'll just blow it off,' he said in a cold voice. James and Amy looked at him. They weren't sure about the turn this had taken. They were mindful that these people were under the control of the devices in their necks, and they had no desire to hurt them or be cruel to them.

Everybody in the lift had been shocked by Simon's actions, but they had the desired effect. The electronic gloves had an 'unlock' code, which allowed them to be freely cloned and passed on, so long as it was authorized by the wearer. James, Simon and Amy each generated a clone and removed the one worn by the guard.

'I'm going to stay behind and get Doctor Pierce's encrypted signal cloned for Magnus,' said Simon. James and Amy looked at him – reluctant – but then nodded. It was the right thing to do. On his own and dressed in the correct uniform now, he'd go unnoticed. And he had the electronic glove.

Amy pressed the buttons in the lift, moving down to Level 4, the location of the hangar. A text message arrived on the Comms-Tabs alerting them that Dan and Nat were on their way there. They had just a few minutes to secure the area for them, to make sure it was clear of guards. That should be okay with the main activity going on around the Troopers one level up.

Kate's guards had been stunned and left unconscious in the lift. Amy and James marched out with Magnus's security team appearing to be prisoners. As they exited, James fully armed his gun and shot the keypads in the lift several times. 'That will slow them down!' he said.

They walked confidently away as if they had every reason to be there. As they encountered Kate's guards, and there were relatively few of them, they stunned them with their weaponry. By the time they'd reached the end of the long corridor, Magnus's team was armed and they were no longer pretending to be prisoners. They were soon in the hangar with the drones.

The electronic gloves gave them access wherever they wanted to go now – at least Kate had helped them in that respect.

Amy was amazed at the sheer size of the area. It seemed incredible that this could be located underground, in a rural part of Scotland, unknown to everybody. All was quiet in the hangar, there were still many unlaunched drones here. Amy shuddered as she pictured hundreds of the things making their way over to the other three bunkers. It was a chilling thought.

There was some activity over on the far side of the hangar: a colourful shimmer of light, and Dan and Nat appeared on the Transporter. Amy would have thought herself to be dreaming only twenty-four hours previously, but she was already beginning to accept this new world in which she was operating.

Nat rushed to the main console in the hangar, replaced the enabling unit, and placed her hand on the activation panel – the same panel that Dan had used earlier, the panel which had allowed Kate to capture and replicate his DNA sequence.

As Nat declared victory, at the precise moment that the enabling unit scrambled the console and re-routed the control sequences to Magnus's terminal in Quadrant 3, Kate's device automatically scanned and recorded Nat's DNA sequence on a console in the Control Room. The sequence that, when combined with Dan's replicated DNA signature, would give unstoppable access to the remaining three Quadrants.

They had to run and get out of the hangar – they'd

already created enough trouble on Level 3 to get Kate's attention. The lift had been disabled, but it would only be a matter of time before they found a way down, bringing some Troopers along this time, no doubt.

They all ran towards the Transporter. Dan and Nat re-activated it immediately, hoping that, if they were interpreting the strange symbols correctly, they would now be taken to Quadrant 2.

Three things happened at the moment of activation. The device which only moments before had harvested Nat's DNA information, replicated it digitally and sent the update remotely to the electronic gloves, updating each one with the new data, including those worn by Amy, Simon and James.

At the moment of activation, James took out his weapon and shot the activation panel to stop Kate's troops following behind them. And on the far side of the hangar, the terminal where the enabling unit had been replaced exploded in a mass of electrical flashes. The cloned model which Magnus had created had successfully transferred all the data necessary for him to permanently disable the remaining drones.

As they re-materialized in Quadrant 2 and made their way along the corridor to the main lift, the small group felt happy with what they'd accomplished. By now they knew not to stop to explore the unfamiliar levels. They needed to open up this area as soon as possible to the Custodian, Viktor. They'd now be able to stop the drones.

They'd disabled the lift and a Transporter on the lowers levels in Quadrant 1, so Kate should not be able to follow behind them. They didn't realize that Kate now had everything that she needed to access all areas of the four Quadrants. Having captured both DNA sequences, like Dan and Nat, there were now no doors closed to her. Her soldiers were assembling on Level 3, now dressed in full combat gear and fully armed. They had given away their only advantage – the unique DNA sequencing of the twins. As the lift made its way up to Level 1 of Quadrant 2, Amy breathed a small sigh of relief as the doors began to slide open. She thought that things could only get better now; events seemed to have turned in their favour.

They were met by Viktor and a group of his armed guards. They raised their weapons which were set to kill. Viktor spoke in a cold, calm, ruthless voice. He was a man used to war. 'Put your weapons down!

'Twins, you must come with me. We have some nuclear submarines to activate.'

PART THREE: THE UNSEEN ENEMY

Chapter One

01:12 Quadrant 4: Dixia Cheng, Beijing

Xiang looked once again at the data on the screen. Her lab team had alerted her to rush over quickly to share what they'd found. She'd been grateful for the distraction – the drones were arriving at regular intervals now, and the violent shaking of the bunker as one after the other launched its missiles was disconcerting and unnerving.

Xiang was on familiar territory in the lab – this was where she preferred to be. The pressures of leadership were not something that she particularly enjoyed, though at certain times in life you have to make choices which are not ideal, but which are necessary. In Xiang's case, to continue to do her ground-breaking work, fully financed and away from prying eyes, she'd had to assume a higher degree of seniority. If she hadn't made these choices, she would not be in the very privileged position of looking at the unbelievable information that was being presented to her on the screen.

If this information was correct, it changed everything that was happening in the four Quadrants. The drones were probably the least of their problems. But when and how should she tell the twins and their parents … if at all?

Xiang was normally a calm and quiet leader, which is why the entire team from the lab – feeling smug with their discovery – jumped into action when Xiang exploded with impatience. 'Check this data again!' she commanded. 'This work is sloppy. Come back to me only when you can confirm these results with a 99 percent or more degree of accuracy!'

The lab team left the room, looking guiltily at each other. They knew that they'd rushed through the results to bring them to Xiang as quickly as they could. In scientific terms, she was correct – they had been sloppy.

But to all intents and purposes the procedures that they'd followed were fairly irrelevant. The simple truth of the data facing Xiang on the screen was so compelling that she knew already it had to be true.

Parted

As far as Nat was concerned, it had just been an ordinary day. She was walking along with Dan, chatting as they did so, and they came to the kerb. They'd stopped there to wait for Amy to catch up with them, so she still wasn't quite clear why she'd stepped ahead into the road.

It all happened so fast. She was sure that Amy had told them to go on ahead, but Dan stepped back suddenly to look at something and Mum's attention was caught by a stranger who distracted her.

The future can spin around on events that occur in a single moment. And so it was for Nat. A black car suddenly accelerated forward towards her and Dan.

Dan stepped back and as he did so avoided being struck by a fraction of a second. Amy had turned to acknowledge the stranger, and in so doing had been unaware of the vehicle that had suddenly veered towards her children. Nat saw something black approaching at speed to the side of her, but then there was a blank in her memory.

The next thing she knew she was aware of a man

crouched over her as she lay in the road. She was in some considerable pain, but he'd just used a device on her that was swiftly taking that pain away. She was aware of panic all around her – a mess of voices – but she could pick out her mum's distinctly. She was crying and in a state of panic.

As quickly as the pain went, she drifted out of consciousness once again and became aware of the man's words fading. Then she fell into a deep sleep.

'I'm so sorry, I can't save her ...'

Nat was aware of nothing else for some time after that. She was alive, because she could dream. Or was this death? Whatever it was, it was fine, only she couldn't wake up. She was able to dream endlessly, and inhabit a world of memories and imagination. But she never seemed to awaken. Try as she might to shake off the dream state and jolt herself out of it, she was unable to do so. She couldn't move her body either. Wherever she was, she was trapped.

01:29 Quadrant 1: Troywood, Fife

Simon was now a free agent. He'd split off from Amy and James and he'd managed to win enough trust to be given one of the SymNodes. He'd seen these before, a few years ago, but the technology had advanced massively since then. He knew that The Global Consortium was experimenting with the glove-like devices to enable them to duplicate fingerprints, and, although they'd had some success, at the time he used them they were still unreliable. The idea was that you could send data directly from a fingerprint database to the glove and 'become' any person that you wanted to be.

Retina identification had become more prevalent in recent times, but these SymNodes seemed to be using a completely different type of technology. They had now managed to link it with DNA. If that's what these things were, you could literally become any person that you wanted to be in terms of gaining access to a building or prohibited area.

Kate was demonstrating the damage that could be done when technology like this falls into the wrong hands. Simon thought about Kate again. He was massively conflicted. He and Kate had been teamed up many years ago on what was his first ever encounter with The Global Consortium. They'd been in the military at the time, both fairly raw recruits, but eagerly volunteering to take part in some essential trials. They'd bonded well as a team, but after the events surrounding the accident, it had been quite clear that they were not to meet again. He'd thought about her often since then and wondered what had happened to her after that terrible day.

He'd gone on to be groomed for The Global Consortium, where he'd worked ever since. He was never quite sure who he was working for or what his work was in aid of, but he knew it to be linked to the Government and the military in some way. The generous pay cheques came in every month, he was constantly given interesting work, he was happy with his lot. Until he'd killed the child.

Kate had not recognized him in the bunker, but he knew her to be a good woman, honest and with integrity. As he made his way to the Operations Centre in order to obtain the encrypted data from Doctor Pierce's secure message, Simon thought carefully about his strategy in these events.

He needed to stop Kate and save her from whatever – or whoever – was making her behave in this way, but he was not going to let her die. He understood enough about The Global Consortium to know that this was what it had all been about all along.

The current events in the Quadrants were what the training, subterfuge and covert operations had been about for all of these years. He'd always been on the edges, never part of the inner circle. Now he was right in the middle of it and having dedicated so many years of his life to this project, he was determined to get to the bottom of it.

Simon was easily able to access the Operations Centre where earlier Dan had received the encrypted messages from Doctor Pierce. The bunker was a big place, and Kate was preoccupied with her new Trooper army. It would not be long before all four levels of Quadrant 1 were fully manned and properly guarded. Using the SymNode glove device, Simon was able to access the console that Dan had used earlier.

All electronics leave a trail and Doctor Pierce's message was no exception. Of course, nobody would ever have found it if they didn't know it was there in the first place – it was only because Dan had shared the information about the private messages that they even knew to look for it in the first place.

Magnus talked Simon through a few procedures via the Comms-Tab. Simon transferred the encrypted code sequence back to Quadrant 3 so that the tech team there could begin an analysis. Once they could speak to Doctor Pierce directly it was possible that things might become a little clearer. Simon looked around the Operations Centre and wondered about its purpose. It had been meant to lie here unused and undiscovered, yet clearly this all had a purpose in the great plan.

He thought back to snippets of information that he'd heard whilst doing routine work for The Global Consortium. Nothing was substantiated, but being around so many Consortium staff for so much of the time, you're bound to hear things that perhaps you're not meant to.

On the screen to the left of the Operations Centre were huge, digital schemata of the bunker. He'd not really got a sense of the shape of the bunkers as he'd been walking through them, other than that there appeared to be four levels, and each level was based around a long corridor which was curved on the lower two levels. The diagrams on the screen made it very clear though. Levels 1 and 2 were rectangular and uniform, built on a simple, grid layout, probably more than half a century ago, Simon supposed. But the two levels below them had a curved edge, as if they were built at a different time – or for a different purpose. 'Quadrants' was the ideal way to describe them.

But there was something more intriguing about the diagrams for Simon. Below the plans for Quadrant 1 were what he assumed must be smaller exploded maps of the remaining three Quadrants. Each was based on the same principle. Only he noticed that each Quadrant was curved differently, so that if joined together they would form an annulus, a huge circular construction.

That was all very well – it made perfect sense to replicate each of the designs wherever the actual buildings were located. But there was a fifth plan which was troubling Simon. This set of diagrams was completely unlike the others. They showed a new area, a hub, which was spherical in shape.

In isolation, none of this information would have been remarkable, but Simon had just realized something that had been staring him in the face since the first day he'd started officially working for The Global Consortium all those years ago. It was concealed in the logo: a square in which was set a circle. The circle was divided into four quadrants and inside the circle was the spherical centre of the entire arrangement. There was another location, and it was at the heart of this entire operation. The Quadrants were just additional parts – the heart was where all the power resided. And if he was piecing together those snippets of overheard conversations correctly, this operational hub was not based on this planet.

It was somewhere above Earth, orbiting in space.

01:32 Quadrant 2: Balaklava Bay, Crimea

We seem to be moving from one bad situation to another. The first thing I looked for when Viktor gave us his surprise greeting was a neck device. Sure enough, he has a faint purple colouring under his skin, but it's not pulsating. The red devices in Quadrant 1 looked like they were working overtime, but Mum's and James's devices are at rest, as were the green Neuronic Devices in Xiang's bunker. Everybody in Viktor's bunker has the devices fitted. Nobody seems to be aware of these things except for us. Magnus is analysing them right now and I'm looking forward to hearing what he has say.

If we get that far.

Viktor has separated us, so Mum and James have been taken off somewhere and Nat and I have been escorted to Level 3 of this bunker. I say 'escorted', but it was more case of Nat and I being coerced to give Viktor and his security team access to the lower levels. He doesn't seem to realize that he could just use the electronic glove devices that Mum and James are using – they're extremely hard to see when they're not activating anything, so I'm guessing that we're best keeping that secret to ourselves for now.

Viktor isn't cruel or unpleasant and we don't appear to be prisoners, but, at the same time, I wouldn't call us welcome guests. He takes us to the Operations Centre, leaving his security team at the lift doors along the curved corridor. Interesting, he doesn't want them with us.

We step inside the Operations Centre. It's a virtual replica of the one in Quadrant 1 where I'd received the secure message from Doctor Pierce. Viktor relaxes once the doors have closed – it's like somebody defrosted him.

'Nat, Dan, welcome to Quadrant 2, Balaklava Bay. I am sorry to be so abrupt with you.'

His English is good, but I can tell that he's speaking with a Russian accent. More knowledge gleaned from TV. Whatever did people do before they had all this knowledge and information right at their fingertips?

These Transporters are incredible – we're hopping all around the world – and we don't even have to suffer in-flight meals.

'I have brought you here because I need your help ... and I have to ask you to trust me.'

Nat exchanges a glance with me. We're not so sure, but we indicate that he should carry on. I've read about a 'poker face' many times in books before, but now I know what it means. I put on my best poker face, so Viktor can't tell what I'm thinking.

'You know that what is happening right now is really serious? And that you twins are very important to the final solution?'

We nod. Nat looks as unconvinced as me that we're going to actually help to solve this current crisis. As if on cue, a drone missile strikes the ground high above us and a rumble resonates throughout the bunker. That must be all three Quadrants now under constant missile attack. New drones will be arriving all the time. We stopped any more launching, but, from the size of that hangar, loads must have already been launched. There is no better reminder of how important all this is than the constant shaking of the Quadrants as each missile finds it target.

'Like Quadrant 1, we have a military capacity in this bunker,' continues Viktor. 'Only I believe that we can use it strategically.

'This bunker is linked to the Black Sea and we are situated within a bay which gives easy water access. I believe that we should launch the submarine drones concealed within these lower levels.' He hesitates for a moment, then continues: 'The submarine drones are armed with nuclear warheads. They are very powerful and can do a lot of damage, much more damage than the drones from Quadrant 1.

'We should be thankful that whoever is sabotaging this operation has not been able to activate or control this base. These submarines are far more dangerous than the air drones.

'Nat and Dan, the reason I need your help is that I cannot activate these submarines without you; they are locked into whatever is special about you two.'

Nat's thinking the same as me. We both just messed up our poker faces. He seems to be saying that Nat and I can activate a nuclear arsenal. I know there have been many concerns expressed about national security in the past, but this one would have the whole world in a state of panic. Mum can't even trust me with the TV remote, let alone a nuclear arsenal.

'I am a military man,' Viktor continues, 'and I know how this situation will play out. If Quadrant 1 gets the upper hand by destroying the remaining Quadrants, there is no way to fight back.

'If we release the submarines, we do not have to launch the missiles, but if they are off this base, hidden beneath the Black Sea, then they may be used later, by us or ...'

He's uneasy now, thinking through another scenario I suspect.

'Or by anybody who is left to fight Quadrant 1.

'I want you to help me to release the submarines, but I promise to give joint control to Xiang and Magnus.

'It may be the only hope that we have against Quadrant 1, and if we have to, it will also allow us to destroy their bunker.'

I feel like somebody should be dialing the Prime Minister. Have they mixed me up for a world leader? Easily done I suppose. Nat and I look at each other. The more time we spend with each other, the more weird it gets. I know what she's thinking already and she knows what I'm thinking. It's not like we have two voices going on in our heads at once – it's more like we have one voice, but we're sharing it. Our answer for Viktor is 'Yes'.

I've seen enough today to know that this is all about options. It's about leaving as many possibilities open as possible. So that as different options close down, we still have some left, places where we can go. To fight, to hide or to re-group. Wriggle room.

Viktor leads us to a panel – he's taken a tablet device out of his pocket to guide him through this process. Nat and I place our hands on a red panel and a digitized map appears on the large screen in front of us. In an instant, what must be well over two hundred dots illuminate on the screen. We know what we just did, and I hope that we made the right decision to trust Viktor. We just armed a fleet of nuclear submarines. And they just started making their way out towards the Black Sea.

Chapter Two

02:02 Quadrant 3: White Sulphur Springs, West Virginia

Magnus braced himself for another violent tremor running throughout the bunker. Every time a missile hit the ground above it could mean the end for this Quadrant, but he tried to remain calm, steady and focused. Nothing ever got achieved by running around in a blind panic. He was assessing the information that he'd just received from the team briefing.

Mike was proving to be a huge asset, though his hacking skills were being tested to the extreme by the files within The Global Consortium mainframe. He'd got through the front door, but essentially found himself in a room with many more locked doors. Each lock needed to be picked.

He'd hesitated for a moment, and couldn't decide whether to go one lock at a time and take pot luck on what was behind each door, or to take the choice which he knew was most sensible: to go for the big picture first. Figure out the system which keeps all the doors locked, then create the individual keys faster.

He made the sensible choice, but would still need to crack the first code to work out the encryption basis for the locking system. Mike had decided to share the work, so five more of Magnus's best tech people had been given wormhole access and let loose on the system. Sooner or later one of them would get that first lock picked.

Mike hadn't felt like this for some time, it was good to be competing against the clock with a team of younger, talented coders. Only he'd been around since most of this code had been invented, so whereas they had to learn it, he knew it already.

Magnus was pleased with Mike's updates, but anxious that they seemed no closer to stopping the drones. There was better news on the neck devices. They were some sort of electronic and biological implant which was able to control certain parts of the brain by, essentially, hijacking the neural pathways in the spine. It appeared that the devices were dormant by default, but that they could be controlled remotely. Nobody within Magnus's bunker had any recollection of these devices being fitted.

Magnus assigned the tech teams two tasks. Firstly, to determine how the devices could be blocked or disabled. Secondly, to figure out where they were being controlled from because, wherever that location was, it would probably help to track down their enemy.

The final part of the briefing came late as the first encryption analysis arrived mid-meeting on Magnus's E-Pad. It was unclear from where Doctor Pierce's secured message had been sent. Several thousand frequencies and channels had been scanned already, but there were many billion possibilities and, even with the amazing technology within the bunker, it took time to check and filter them all.

However, something had been very clear even from this basic analysis. The message had been sent on a frequency via the X-Band. Although it was not yet certain, that was a very strong indicator that Doctor Pierce's message had not been sent from one of the four Quadrants. Most likely it had been sent from space.

Global Consortium Simulation Centre (9 October 2000)

Kate and Simon were trapped in a room which was being attacked from all sides. They were out of breath, hot and in a heightened state of anxiety. Only minutes ago they'd been awoken at their mission destination. The location had to remain top secret, so they'd been restored to full consciousness just outside the electrified wire fence.

It had all gone according to plan for the first few minutes, then the Stealth-Shields had deactivated, as if there had been a sudden power failure. The orientation in the building was all wrong, weapons had been fired at them and they'd ended up trapped in this room – confronted by an array of screens.

On each screen was a live feed of various loved ones: Simon's mum and dad, working in the garden; Kate's older sister, studying at her desk at university; Kate's mum, visiting the grave of her dad; Simon's brother, sitting in a coffee shop reading the paper. Each person had a target resting on them.

The instructions had been clear. Either they must accept death or their family members must perish. Observing the simulation in the gallery, a man watched the screen nervously, hoping that they'd make the right decision. He'd only just managed to fend off the attacks and the criticisms after the simulation that had gone badly wrong earlier in the year. His position was assured for now, but any more errors and it was unlikely that he'd remain at the helm of this project.

Statistically, he knew what would happen, as it did well over 99.9 percent of the time. But he'd lost some self-confidence now, and this was the stage where he always became agitated. Most people made their decision by the time the countdown had reached three seconds – two seconds at the very latest.

Zero–97/4 and Zero–98/4 – the troublesome test subjects – had made their decision at one second to go in the countdown. The countdown now was on two seconds remaining.

This couple had worked well as a team. They had bonded in battle instantly, finding a level of communication and understanding in the heat of an intense drama. Two seconds – Simon and Kate looked at each other. One second – a small nod of understanding. He cursed as he watched the monitor, this was the second team to go to the one-second point, it meant only one thing.

Only he was wrong. The problem with human beings is that they're unpredictable. Statistics will tell you how most of them will behave in a certain situation. But with free will comes individuality, and Simon and Kate – or Ten–32/7 and Ten–32/8 as they would be referred to in the test results – had decided to assert their free will in a completely different way.

James and Amy played for time, both sustaining injuries in the process. Simon and Kate did something equally courageous and unpredictable. They called their tormentors' bluff. They laid down their weapons, sat on the floor, and stared at their persecutors on the monitor cameras. 'We refuse to make a choice!' shouted Simon.

The simulation team were so sure that all the results could be statistically predicted, they were taken completely unawares. The main laser console in the room powered up and locked in on both of them. The troops at the door burst into the room and levelled their weapons, ready to fire. The targets on the screens began a five-second countdown, the remote assassins ready to annihilate their family members.

Kate and Simon held steady, uncertain if they had just condemned themselves and their families to death. There was an urgent electronic sound, which they assumed was the laser powering up … then, nothing. The monitor screens disappeared. The soldiers and the laser gun in the ceiling disappeared. The troops who had been pounding on the windows disappeared.

They were in a massive hangar space which was marked out by row upon row of green grid lines. They thought they were alone but both were suddenly aware of movement at the far end of the hangar area.

In the brief moment before they were rendered unconscious by laser fire, both Kate and Simon just had time to realize that whatever it was that they were looking at, it certainly wasn't human.

Experiments

For much of the three years that Nat had been away from her family, she'd been asleep, kept in a state of permanent stasis in a pod of the same type used in the bunkers. She'd been woken and put to sleep, then woken and put to sleep again. She had not been aware of the passage of time, except when she was awake and the experiments were being carried out.

Nobody ever spoke to her. There were no words of comfort, no explanation as to what was going on. Bit by bit, she accumulated information about her situation.

Firstly, she was sure that she wasn't dead, though if there was a Hell, it might have been something like this. Secondly, one man was in charge here – he held a lot of power and the people around him were extremely frightened of him. Thirdly, whatever it was that they were after from her, they were struggling to get it.

The man in charge would be furious after the experimentation sessions. There was a secret locked deep inside her that he was trying to access, but, for whatever reason, it was eluding him.

It took her several months to piece together these

fragments of information. She would have a few minutes after being woken, and she would compel herself to remember, in spite of the pain of the tests.

They would lay her on a cold, metal operating table. She was unable to move: she had recovered full consciousness after stasis, but they obviously needed her stunned and docile so that she couldn't run away. She would be left there for hours at a time sometimes.

No thought was given to her comfort, no food or drink was offered. She never felt hungry or thirsty, so she assumed that whatever happened in the pod between these horrible sessions took care of all of that. If only there was something to manage the fear and the dread.

When an experiment began, it would be triggered by a large device being positioned at the side of the operating table, not unlike something that you might see at the dentist. It would start with a whirr – the medical staff would leave the room and only the man would be left in the adjacent room, monitoring panels and screens as if his own life depended on them.

At hourly intervals, for a twenty-four hour period, needles would be placed at angles in four places at the base of her spine. They would inject some kind of fluid or serum – she could feel it shooting up her spine and into her brain. It was the final fluid that she dreaded most of all. It put her in agonizing spasms until the process began once again on the hour, every hour, twenty-four hours in a row each time.

By the time she was put back in stasis she was desperate for the relief that sleep would bring. There was one thing that got her through this excruciating torture, one piece of information which she was determined above all else would remain etched on her brain whatever happened.

It was the name that she was compelled to look at as this inhumanity was administered, the wording that was clearly displayed on the lapel badge attached to his white lab coat. It read 'Dr H. Pierce'.

As the letters burned an indelible image on the back of her retina, she vowed to herself that she would escape this place and make sure this man was punished for what he had done to her.

02:07 Quadrant 2: Balaklava Bay, Crimea

Viktor watched the dots on the E-Pad screen as they moved towards the exit of Quadrant 2. On the level below them, in an area which they had not yet seen, the submarine drones were activating one by one in the chamber that was buried deep within the bay. It operated like a vast, iron lock, water being drawn from beyond the bunker to bring the chamber up to sea level so that the submarines could be released.

As each one activated, two lights glowed red in the darkness. Once more, the eyes of a devil. The submarines would be moved up to sea level, then a force field would be activated to allow them to enter the Black Sea without letting the darkness outside permeate the bunker. Each one had to traverse a long, dimly lit channel which led out into the sea beyond.

Like the airborne drones, they would leave the bunker at regular intervals, travelling below the surface to assume their positions deep under the waters beyond. At the appointed time they could rise nearer to the surface to release their armoury of nuclear missiles.

Nat and Dan had colluded with Viktor to enable

this release because they believed it to be in the best interests of everybody involved. What Viktor had said made complete sense. He had been as good as his word – once Dan and Nat had activated the subs, he'd notified Xiang and Magnus and given them joint control via a remote and secure connection. But he'd omitted one crucial piece of information.

Two hundred submarines were being released from the base, one at a time, each one of them under the joint control of Viktor, Magnus and Xiang. No missile could be released without the agreement of all three Custodians.

What Viktor hadn't mentioned were the fifty subs currently being activated with a different tracking encryption. These were armed with nuclear missiles just like the others and they would sit patiently under the Black Sea awaiting further remote commands. These subs required only one authorization, thanks to Nat and Dan having just granted top level access.

Viktor alone was needed to activate these nuclear missiles and that was a secret that he intended to keep from everybody.

Chapter Three

Dissent

He had not felt this level of hostility since he had been forced to defend the outcome of the failed simulations earlier that year. In each of the cases, he'd had to fight to maintain his position within The Global Consortium.

He was playing a difficult game here – there were so many parties to appease and they were all intent on achieving their own outcomes from the Genesis 2 project. He'd also managed to keep all four of the troublemakers in his sights, unknown to the members of The Consortium.

For the partners in the project, they were a big problem. They'd all seen and done things that had not been anticipated. Amy went on with her civilian life, but he'd managed to assign to her the most important role, one which it was likely she'd finally realize as a result of the events unfolding now. It was a secret that was hiding in the open, his preferred strategy.

James had returned to the military where he could be monitored closely – ready when he needed him, maintaining his fitness and training. Triggering him for redundancy, then placing the new job opportunity in front of him – it had been easy and predictable where James was concerned.

Simon had proven an excellent recruit, and had done many years of fine work on behalf of The Consortium. Now his role was completed, he wouldn't be a part of the endgame.

Then there was Kate. She'd had an interesting career, away from the glare of The Consortium, separated from Simon, but placed exactly where he could see her. He was completely sure of her leadership qualities, which was why the current state of affairs in Quadrant 1 was so worrying to him. Kate was a massive military asset – but it depended on which side she was on as to whether that was to your advantage or not. In this case, she was definitely not the person that you would want to have fighting against you.

Reluctantly, he'd had to admit to the world leaders angrily seeking answers from him in his Ops Area high above the Earth that he'd concealed some facts from them after those botched simulations. He'd also had to notify them of Kate's activation and deployment of the Troopers.

There was certainly a lot of hostility towards him as he bargained and pleaded with the near two hundred angry faces surrounding him on the screens. But as their votes came in, and were tallied one by one on the screen, it was clear to him that he was no longer in control here, The Global Consortium was now ignoring his advice.

Their responses were given via direct access to their consciousness. They were represented before him only by holographic images, but their authority was final in these matters. He was just the one orchestrating these events, as he had done for many years now, yet he was the one who could best predict how this was all going to play out.

But the votes were in. When it went to a full ballot, he had no say. They had opted for the most extreme response. They'd actually sanctioned Unification.

02:24 Quadrant 3: White Sulphur Springs, West Virginia

Magnus studied the data that had just arrived on his E-Pad. This was technology that he understood – it was advanced and very clever, yes, but he could deal with this. He was working through the analysis on the neck implants.

It seemed likely that whatever had caused Kate's bunker to sabotage the Genesis 2 project was related in some way to these implants. Nobody had any recollection of them having been put there in the first place, and they couldn't be felt under the skin. Only some of them appeared to be active and they were different colours, dependent on the Quadrant location.

And there was one thing that was particularly mysterious. James and Amy were unique in that they were the only ones with a blue implant.

They appeared to be based on biotechnology. The devices were essentially electronic in nature – in the way that they transmitted and received data remotely – but they were enmeshed in each person's brain function, controlling memory, emotion and consciousness. They could rewire a person's thinking once activated.

As far as the tech teams could establish, there were no mind wipes going on; it was a much more subtle process which each individual would find very hard to detect. There were three key pieces of information that the research teams had established from their initial tests.

Firstly, the implants used advanced nanotechnology of a type not recognized by anybody in this Quadrant. Magnus decided to forward the data to Xiang in Quadrant 4 – she'd probably have a better idea as to its source.

Secondly, it was likely that the implants had been put in place during basic training and mission preparation. They were so small that they could easily be inserted as part of a simple and routine procedure, such as taking a blood sample.

Finally, by monitoring the almost imperceptible broadcast trail emitted by each device, Magnus was able to figure out how the implants were receiving data. Each device was in a constant state of readiness, emitting a faint pulse which was capable of receiving data from a source which was, as yet, unknown.

This source had to be separate from any other communications within the bunker itself. They had been designed to give remote control of bunker staff in a way that was not dependent on any of the other technology. They appeared to be a fail-safe. But in this situation, the fail-safe had been hijacked to create a direct route to control the actions of the bunker staff in Quadrant 1.

Mixed among all the tech and unanswered questions was some good news. The data received by the implants was being transmitted via a fairly old fashioned system. Whoever invented these devices needed an external system for relaying the data around the world. They'd used the existing mobile phone network. Rather than build their own network of aerials, they'd simply piggy-backed off an existing global facility. Hiding in the open, where everybody could see them, but nobody actually did.

To prevent the signals reaching Quadrant 1, they'd have to blow up the mobile mast placed only a couple of hundred yards away from the cottage which concealed the bunker. There was a chance that there might be a signal breakthrough from other transmitters, but Magnus thought it unlikely. If they could just break that signal to Quadrant 1, they might at least stop fighting each other and work together to resolve the issue of the drones.

There was one man who had already operated the doors in Quadrant 1, who knew the way out of that bunker – it was James. And in the debrief, Simon had revealed the Consortium technology that he'd been wearing which had enabled him to see beyond the bunker doors, in spite of the darkness outside.

Another drone missile exploded on the surface, high above Magnus. It violently shook the whole bunker, spilling Magnus's coffee which had been resting on the side of the table. He would need to move fast. Finally, they had the means to break Kate's hold on the first Quadrant.

As Magnus quietly celebrated this small victory alone in Quadrant 3, Kate was finishing the final briefing in her own bunker. Her army of Troopers stood before her, motionless, threatening, heavily armed and mission ready. Over their eyes were complex electronic visors, attached to menacing, black helmets – these would enable them to see in any environment, including the darkness beyond their own bunker doors. They were heavily armed, with multi-barrelled laser attachments on one arm, and multiple weapons in their body armour. Each wore a SymNode, the very device that could now give them access to any level in any of the Quadrants which had already been accessed by the twins. And, as Kate spoke, the black implants in their necks pulsed steadily, receiving data from an unknown source far away.

These troops were instruments of war and if Magnus had known the mission that they had just been given, he might not have been quite so pleased with himself.

Within a matter of only hours, the Troopers had been instructed to overcome and secure each of the remaining Quadrants, making Kate the sole Custodian of them all.

Change

The Shards were all in place now, doing the regenerative work that had to be done to save the planet. This was how Earth would be healed, and like a patient who had to be put to sleep during a difficult and delicate operation, so it was for the inhabitants of this planet.

They would eventually awaken, unaware of what had been going on around them, oblivious to how close they were to destroying the very environment which was supposed to sustain them.

There was a sudden change in the activity of the Shards. They had been dispatched from the satellite matrix which surrounded the Earth and, up to this point, they had been under the control of that matrix. But something unexpected was happening now.

Where once the Shards pulsed blue, green, purple and yellow, that gentle and reassuring rhythm ceased momentarily, as if the heart which gave them life had just stopped beating. The pulse began once again, but the Shards were different now. The colour which once flowed through them had gone. The Shards had become dark, black and menacing.

They beat slowly and portentously, like the threatening thunderous footfall of an approaching army intent on destruction.

Incarceration

Nat had no choice but to endure the experimentation in the lab. She could not cry for help. Nobody knew that she was there. She was completely defenceless against her jailers.

But as her life slipped into a nightmarish routine of experimentation and deep sleep, she noticed that the man in charge was becoming more agitated. As he became more agitated, he grew more angry, increasingly unpredictable, and most importantly, careless.

She felt as if she was constantly fighting sleep and pain, but she knew that to stand any chance of escape, she had to stay aware, she had to watch and spot the patterns. If she knew how people moved, what they did, when they did it and how, she would eventually be able to figure a way out of this Hell.

Some things that she saw were so bizarre, she wondered if they were part of her dreams. The people here seemed to speak through devices attached to their hands, and she was sure that once she'd even seen somebody materialize out of thin air, surrounded by an amazing array of shimmering lights. She could not be sure sometimes what was real and what was not.

Nat had been in the Lab for almost two years when she finally spotted her chance. Her muscles were wasting from lack of activity, she knew that she would need to find her strength before she could attempt an escape. She'd watched, learned and struggled to remember between periods of stasis. She'd fought to focus on that information as the agonizing serums had been injected into her spinal column. It had taken her two years of this treatment to piece together the fragments.

The pod was always unlocked. It was the stasis that left her immobile and sleeping – the pod didn't need to be locked when she was held in that state. The stasis came via direct contact with electrodes attached to her head. If she could break the contact, she could stop the stasis.

The area where her pod was kept was under camera surveillance. The camera swept the room. It fixed on the pod for three seconds, took ten seconds to cover the length of the room, then it paused for three seconds, then another ten seconds back to the pod. That gave her twenty-three seconds to get behind the pod, away from the camera.

Then she got her break. One of the lab team dropped a wrapper on the floor. She stood on it when being moved from the pod to the table. It stuck to her foot. She strained her body to grab it while the staff calibrated the instrumentation. This was going to act as her insulation between the electrodes and the pod.

The staff were as much in a routine as she was, but that played to her advantage. They weren't expecting her to move, to run, to try anything – after all, she had been in stasis, she was pretty well useless. So nobody was expecting her to do or try anything – and that was her opportunity.

It took every bit of will that Nat could muster to progress her plans. She craved the stasis when they placed her back in the pod, because that was the only thing that brought relief from the experimentation. But she forced herself to place the torn wrapper across the electrodes as the staff prepared the pod around her.

She would watch and count, fighting the pain. The camera would move off the pod. The staff would check the machine, calibrate her food, vitamin and liquid intake to prepare for stasis. Nat would adjust the electrodes in that short window while the camera was scanning the rest of the room and the staff were busy elsewhere.

The first time she tried it she braced herself as the gushing sound which preceded stasis swept through the pod. The electrical hum began. She was still awake. Every part of her body craved sleep, but she had to force herself through this, or it would never end.

For a while she waited, working through her pain and discomfort. She had no idea how long they kept her in stasis. The doctor worked long hours, constantly in that office of his, swiping away at the terminal, talking to somebody via a communications device at regular intervals. Reporting his results, or so it seemed to her. When he finally finished, she was left alone. And awake.

She pushed the door of the pod as the camera was turned away – it opened easily, unlocked as she'd previously figured out. She waited for the camera to make its next sweep. Her legs were weak, she hadn't done any sustained walking for … she didn't know how long she'd been in there. She had body strength though and it was obviously important to them that she was kept fed through her tubes. The tubes. She slipped them off one by one, and tensed her arms and legs. She had to know that they were going to work properly when she needed them to.

The camera made its sweep once again. It was now or never. She started her count.

One … two … three …

She opened the door to the pod and stepped out.

Her legs held her weight, but she was unsteady. They always supported her by her arms on the short walk to the operating table.

Seven … eight … nine …

She quietly closed the door to the pod.

Fourteen … fifteen … sixteen …

She was aware of the camera resting for three seconds and now pointing at the other end of the room. She'd need to move fast.

Nat stepped behind the pod, pushing herself harder than she'd ever thought she could go, fighting the pain that ran through her body, willing her legs to move properly to take her to where she needed to hide. She'd been right. There was an area behind the pod where she could position herself completely away from the camera. Here was where she would prepare for her breakout.

She'd never worried about exercise or fitness before, but now it was going to be her only friend as she plotted her escape. Slowly, painfully, she began to stretch and move her legs. Then she moved her arms. It felt amazing to have that freedom of movement once again.

Nat worked through her pain to begin the exercise regime that would eventually lead to her freedom. She was scared at first, not sure how long the stasis lasted. When would the doctor be back? She didn't know, but she needed to stay alert.

It turned out they'd left her for almost a week at a time. Nat counted six days. She was completely alone for six whole days.

On the first few days she'd return to the pod at 6 a.m. in case the doctor began his work early – like a vampire returning to the coffin before sunrise. She'd wait, perfectly still, for a couple of hours, then venture out once again at about 10 o'clock. At the slightest noise, she'd wait for the camera to begin its sweep across the room, then position herself back in the pod in case somebody had returned to the lab.

Bit by bit, Nat gained strength and confidence. But it was two steps forward and one step back every time. They'd leave her for six full days before resuming their tests. Then she'd have to endure twenty-four hours of tests once again.

It took her another three months to firmly establish her new routine. Every time she left the pod, she'd have to force herself through the excruciating pain after the experiments.

But her strength and resilience was building all the time. Every six days she'd get a little stronger and a little braver. And, like a timid mouse venturing beyond the walls of a pantry, she eventually got the courage to explore beyond her cell.

That was when she discovered what all of this testing had been about.

Chapter Four

Mission

Simon received a message from Magnus via his Comms-Tab. He was to remain in Quadrant 1, ready to team up with James. They'd need to make their way to the top level and get to the bunker entrance. From there, James would need to repeat whatever process he'd used to get Amy, Nat and Simon into the bunker in the first place. Then he'd have to blow up that mobile mast.

Magnus had relayed the same message to the other bunkers. Xiang and Viktor would need to assign the same task to security team personnel in their own bunkers. Although their bunker teams had not yet had their Neuronic Devices hijacked, it made sense to pre-empt that possibility, and disable the means of sabotage. For Magnus and Viktor, based in rural locations, it was not so problematical. There was one main mast which was serving each bunker. For Xiang, located deep below Beijing, there were multiple masts to deal with.

The drones may well have damaged some of them, but to defend each bunker from an assault via the neck devices, the mobile networks had to be taken out. Simon decided to keep the information about the bunker layout schemata to himself for now – he wasn't quite sure what it all meant. This spherical construction was worrying him, but he didn't know yet how it would all fit together. He captured some images via his Comms-Tab but didn't share them. They could wait for later, until he had some more information.

He was about to leave the Operations Centre when the main console where he'd been working previously hummed into life. It was his boss, Doctor Pierce, on the screen. 'Dan, are you there?' came his voice.

Simon hesitated, then decided to make himself known. A quick analysis of his situation told him that he could only get closer to the truth by talking to Doctor Pierce, he couldn't end up in much more danger.

'It's me, Simon ...' he began. Then Doctor Pierce's face appeared on the screen.

'Press the green button, third along,' Doctor Pierce continued. 'Give me a visual on you.'

Simon did as he was told, and a two-way video

channel opened.

'Authenticate yourself please,' asked Doctor Pierce, and Simon placed his hand on the panel on the desk.

This was standard Global Consortium procedure. Once satisfied that it really was Simon, Doctor Pierce visibly relaxed.

'I'm not even going to ask how you got there Simon,' said Doctor Pierce, 'but I'm really pleased that you are. We desperately need a man on the inside. There are so many unexpected things happening today, I need some people I can trust.'

'But can I trust you?' Simon thought to himself.

'What's the mission status?' asked Simon, deciding to get whatever information he could.

'Quadrant 1 has been sabotaged,' Doctor Pierce explained. 'This should be impossible, but it's happened. The power should have come on in the bunkers much earlier, but I think it was sabotaged to enable some re-routing of essential channels while we were at our most vulnerable.

'The drones are causing extensive damage – my projections indicate that Quadrant 3 will be the first to suffer structural damage, then Beijing will be second. There's already very extensive drone damage to the city above ground, simulations suggest over sixteen thousand lives lost or at risk so far.'

Simon frowned. This was destruction on a massive scale. Below ground, shielded by the bunkers, it was easy to forget the world outside.

'Kate has activated the Troopers, Simon. Once they're set loose it's going to be extremely difficult for you to get ahead of this thing.'

Doctor Pierce hesitated and looked earnestly into

the camera.

'Simon, we've reached a critical point in this operation. If the Troopers control the Quadrants, there's very little any of us will be able to do.

'I have to warn you though that you need to be ready ...'

Another pause, as if he was deciding whether to share the information or not.

'I've initiated Unification Simon.

'I need to explain what it does.

'You only have forty-five minutes until it's all over.'

02:27 Quadrant 2: Balaklava Bay, Crimea

I'm very uneasy about what we did with the submarines, but I keep thinking it through, and I have come to the conclusion that Viktor handed over joint control to Magnus and Xiang so we have a fail-safe in place – he can't act alone. I have to stop worrying this particular knot, the missiles from the drones are shaking this base at regular intervals now, they won't let us forget what our primary objective should be.

Magnus wants us back in Quadrant 3, he needs James back in Quadrant 1. Mum wants to go with him. They've got to blow up a phone mast just outside Quadrant 1.

Simon only has one protective mask, so it's decided that James should go as he has opened the main bunker doors already. He can't fully recall what he was doing at the time he rescued Mum and Nat, but he dredges his memory and believes that he can work out what to do from the training he received prior to entering the bunker.

Mum isn't happy that he's going alone, especially after all he's been through, but she sees the logic in it. James arms himself and heads for the lift. His plan is to meet Simon at the Operations Centre on Level 3 and they'll make for the blast doors of Quadrant 1 together.

Viktor has suggested that we place armed guards at all known Transporter areas now, and that's agreed by everybody. We know that Kate has assembled some kind of army in Quadrant 1, but we don't know yet what her plan is or what she intends to do next. If we can blow up the mast, we may never need to find out, as Magnus is sure we can disable the neck devices that way.

I suggest that Viktor, Xiang and Magnus search their Level 3 areas – in Quadrant 1 there was lots of equipment there. If Simon has some protective visor for whatever lies beyond the blast doors, I'm betting there's something similar in those areas. That's if their Quadrants are equipped the same as Kate's of course.

We're deciding on the next course of action to take when there's an urgent message from Xiang in Quadrant 2. I've not seen her like this before. She struck me as quiet and even a little shy on our first meeting. Now she's assertive and straight to the point.

'Dan and Nat, I must talk with you and your parents as soon as possible, it's extremely urgent.'

Nat and I look at each other. We suspect Xiang has found something from the tests that she's been running and we're not really sure that we want to learn the results.

'Viktor and Magnus also need to be present.'

'What's going on?' asks Viktor, but he doesn't get a reply.

'Just get to Quadrant 3 as soon as you can,' replies Xiang. 'Our lives depend on it.'

Ally

The days for Nat were long and tedious. She would exercise as much as possible, every day gaining strength and confidence. But she soon realized that this was just prolonging her imprisonment. She had to step beyond the walls of her jail and venture outside. There must be a way for her to leave this place.

She had long periods just standing in the pod, allowing the tubes to feed and nourish her – she had no other source of food. She could see from her reflection in the partition glass that she was looking stronger and more muscular now, so she made an extra effort to appear weak and more helpless every time they moved her back to the operating table.

It was the same every seven days. The medical team would arrive and set up their equipment. Doctor Pierce would take his position through the glass partition, snapping at the other staff, intimidating them, belittling them, even using a taser device on them at times and generally creating a horrible, threatening environment for everybody.

One day, one of the men in his team dropped a vial of whatever it was they were injecting into her, right in front of the pod. Nat watched, motionless and fearful, as Doctor Pierce stormed through into the room. He threw the man onto the floor, screamed at him and grabbed a syringe from the operating table ready to plunge it into his temple. The man was terrified and in fear for his life. The other staff just put their heads down and carried on, not daring to intervene.

Doctor Pierce wouldn't stop. He had pure hatred in his eyes. He just kept shouting at the man, who assumed a foetal position on the ground so as not to intimidate the doctor any further.

Nat thought he was unstable. The way he responded to a simple accident was completely out of proportion. When it was all over and Doctor Pierce had returned to his own office, the man cautiously stood up, leaning on Nat's pod to steady himself as he did so.

Nat hardly dared breathe. His face was level with hers. The man looked completely broken. This was Nat's chance. He wanted to be out of this place as much as she did. Whatever the deal was with Doctor Pierce, handing your notice in was not an option.

She took a leap of faith. If she had gambled incorrectly, how much worse could things get? They'd just make sure that she was in stasis, figure out how she'd blocked the electrodes. When you do the worst thing imaginable to somebody, you don't really have many places to go when it comes to threats. And Nat knew that they needed her alive. She was there to be a lab rat for Pierce.

As the man drew level with her, she moved her eyes to meet his. They looked at each other for a fraction of a second – nobody could have seen it. But he caught Nat's glance and he knew that she'd seen what had happened. He knew too that if she'd worked out a way to beat that terrible man and avoid stasis, she could help him too.

So he gave a small nod of confirmation. Nothing that could be detected on the cameras if anybody was even looking. In that moment Nat had found herself an ally. A man who'd come to this country illegally to try to better himself. A man who'd studied as a scientist in his own country only to be sold as a slave abroad, caught in a role from which there was no escape or release. A man who had every bit as much reason to hate Doctor Pierce as Nat did.

Together they could form an alliance which might finally get her out of this place. An alliance which would ultimately give her the opportunity that she needed to take her final revenge on the spiteful torturer.

Chapter Five

Quadrant 2: Balaklava Bay, Crimea (Unification: T-minus 27 minutes)

The team was assembled ready to transport over to Quadrant 3 where Magnus was waiting. Viktor knew that now was the time he needed to find an excuse to slip away. This was the point at which he would secure his advantage.

'Excuse me,' he said, interrupting the expectant chatter as the group prepared to enter the Transporter. 'I will need to join you shortly, there is a small matter that I need to attend to first.'

Everybody was more pre-occupied with the forthcoming briefing from Xiang and the latest updates from Magnus to be particularly concerned by this. The main group of Amy, Dan and Nat, along with some of Viktor's top team, transported over to Quadrant 3.

Viktor moved down to the Operations Centre on the third level, an area he'd had no time to explore fully yet. He knew what he was looking for though. Already there were personnel down here, exploring the hidden levels now that they had access to the SymNodes, courtesy of Kate. They'd secured the visual and breathing equipment that they needed to destroy the mobile phone mast on the surface above them, the security team were sending him regular E-Pad updates on the progress of that operation.

Viktor headed for the main console, used the SymNode to create the required authorization, and typed some codes into the screen. There was a deep rumble throughout the bunker, caused by the latest drone missile strike high above him on the surface. He had just transferred launch access rights directly to his E-Pad.

Wherever he was now, he could activate the submarine drones if he needed to including the fifty which were in his sole control. It was just a little insurance, depending on how things played out next.

Viktor made his way along the corridor to the nearest Transportation Area. As he activated the unit, he heard a lot of noise going on outside, as if somebody was firing weapons.

He hesitated to complete the transportation process and his hand hovered over the main panel, unsure whether to investigate further or leave it in the hands of his security team. He was just about to step off the Transporter when two of Kate's Troopers burst through the door. Viktor placed his hand on the panel and activated it immediately, just in time to avoid a violent blast of weapon fire.

It looked like he was going to need those nukes after all.

Escape

His name was Dae-Ho and he'd escaped from North Korea. More accurately, he'd been lured by Doctor Pierce from North Korea, targeted for his medical skills, but abused and exploited in exchange for travel papers and a false identity. Threats were made to his family back home if he didn't comply. The man had no choice but to do as he was told.

He crept back into the lab at night, after the latest round of tests. Nat had been alerted when she'd heard him approaching down the corridor. She'd almost got caught by the camera in her panic to conceal herself once again in the pod. She was relieved to see Dae-Ho enter the room, though they had not had a chance to talk yet. As he opened up the pod to speak to Nat, she blurted out in panic about the cameras.

'Disabled,' he smiled. 'They are on a repeating loop: they look like they're sweeping the room, but they're showing an image from an hour ago. We have that long to speak.'

They made their introductions and exchanged their stories. Dae-Ho apologized for what they'd been forced to do to Nat.

'We smuggled in anaesthetic to ease the pain for you,' he said, 'but it's why Pierce is so angry all the time. It skews his results and just makes him experiment more. I honestly believe that man is insane.'

Nat hated to think what the experiments would have been like without anaesthetic. And she'd seen enough of Doctor Pierce to see how things were in this place. These people were terrified of him – he was a violent and unstable man. Over the following weeks, Nat and Dae-Ho plotted their escape plan.

Dae-Ho and the other medical staff were contained in the same building as Nat. They had no freedom of movement and they were still prisoners. Their living quarters were basic, the food they were given minimal and the sanitation and hygiene limited. However, they'd worked out how to get out of the building at night and one of their team had negotiated safe passage to the USA in exchange for giving North Korean secrets. Their escape would be coordinated with an extraction of their families from North Korea. It required careful planning and a set date and time over several time zones. They just had to pick their time and their day, and they had to ensure that it was done without alerting the UK authorities. So it was agreed that Nat would be part of that escape plan. She would leave when the others did. Dae-Ho did not tell the others that Nat would be joining them, he felt it best to maintain the pretence with Doctor Pierce as well as they could.

Nat grew stronger. It was almost three years since the accident and she'd been fully conscious for most of the past year, yet she was sick of the experiments, she didn't know how long she could go on, knowing that escape was so close.

She was almost her normal self now, but however strong her body was the experiments always set her back. Dae-Ho added as much anaesthetic as he dared to, but both were terrified of Doctor Pierce discovering the plan.

It wasn't long until Nat grew more inquisitive about what lay beyond her room. She wanted to know how much of what she'd seen was real, how much semi-conscious hallucination. As she grew stronger and increasingly confident, and as she began to trust Dae-Ho's disabling of the security system more and more, Nat ventured beyond her prison. Dae-Ho would leave her early, with sometimes an hour or thirty minutes buffer time still left on the security camera loop, so she had an opportunity to explore.

One night, two days after the latest batch of experiments, she noticed that Pierce had left his screens on in his work area through the glass partition. He must have done this in error, usually the room was cleared out after the tests. But it looked like this was something different. Nat cautiously stepped out of her room, keying in the code that Dae-Ho had left with her. She checked for cameras along the corridor, but Dae-Ho had assured her that she was clear for another half hour yet.

Alert to the slightest sound, Nat moved quietly towards the next door and entered Doctor Pierce's office. His terminal was still live. It looked as though he'd left it performing an automated operation. She noticed that the video channel was still on – whoever he talked to in here seemed to be monitoring his screen live from a remote location.

Nat stood to the side so that she wouldn't be picked up on the camera, and she held her breath, terrified that she might already have given away her presence.

After waiting for what seemed like hours, she dared once again to look at the console. Doctor Pierce was collating whatever data he'd managed to extract from his endless experiments on her.

She didn't know what it meant, but she could see that whatever it was that he was doing related to the four liquids that were injected into her spinal column during the tests. Something that she hadn't even thought about was that he was also monitoring her responses after the tests. In the six days after each series of experiments, he was monitoring her recovery times day-by-day, hour-by-hour.

She stopped for a moment and thought it through. She broke out into a sweat as she realized the truth of the situation. Doctor Pierce had known what she was up to. He must have seen it in the results. He must have known that she was breaking out of the pod – but did he know the extent of her freedom, and that Dae-Ho was involved? If so, they were all in danger.

A text message popped up on Doctor Pierce's console. At first it was an indecipherable array of unusual symbols. Line by line the symbols were translated into English and Nat watched as the sentences unfolded.

'That's all the information we'll need,' it began. 'I'm transferring over all the data now. You're finished with the girl. Close down the test centre and ensure that there is no evidence left behind.

'You'll need to deliver the girl to us. I'm sure that there's still a lot we can learn from some more thorough experimentation. When we've completed that process, we'll dispose of her.

'You need to prepare to relocate to the Ops Area now, Genesis 2 is beginning in the next fortnight.

'Confirmed that the initial breach will be at Troywood Bunker 15:00 on 15/03, all systems are in place. Confirmed that the Tracy family will be there. I have the codes too.

'Will speak again at the meeting point, Zadra Nurmeen.'

Nat had a lot of new information to assimilate quickly. The tests were over. Doctor Pierce must have known what she was up to all along. It looked like whoever was at the other end of this PC had received all the data that they needed for now. Only it wasn't finished for Nat, they had more tests planned for her.

At that moment, another message popped up on the screen, this time it must have been Doctor Pierce replying from his remote PC.

'Clearing the building shortly. Will get ready to transport the girl. Shutting this terminal down now you have what you need.

'They won't know what hit them, Pierce.'

Whatever Doctor Pierce had planned for this building, it was happening now. She had to warn Dae-Ho, but first she was going to save what she could from the PC. Her mobile phone and various other bits that they'd taken from her pockets were discarded in a cardboard box at the side of his desk. The phone was dead, but Nat took out the SD card and quickly erased her images. She grabbed as much as she could from Doctor Pierce's files and saved it to the disk. The operation was interrupted as the PC was closed down remotely, just as Pierce had said it would be.

Nat ran out into the corridor, unafraid of cameras or being detected now. She was running for her life. If she didn't escape now, she was certain that she never would. Dae-Ho was approaching her from the end of the corridor, stumbling and struggling to move himself forward. Nat ran up to him.

'Nat, I'm so sorry, they have gassed us.

'Take this money, it is South Korean won, it will help you. You must get far away from here Nat. Use the window near the store room, the code is 4897k.'

Dae-Ho collapsed on the floor in front of her. He was completely still, and she knew that he must be dead. She grabbed the currency, ran along the corridor, found the store room and typed the code into the panel. 4897j if she recalled correctly.

No response. Through the glass she could see two black cars pulling up outside. Eight armed men got out and started walking towards the facility entrance. Nat was sure the numbers were right, had she misheard? She heard the door opening further along the corridor.

4897a … 4897k … she was in! Nat leapt through the window just as the sound of footsteps could be heard approaching along her corridor. She quietly closed the window so it would take them longer to work out how she'd made her exit.

She ran as fast as she could, through fields, woodland and along tracks until she finally came to a main road. She waved down a lorry, jumped into the cab before the driver even had a chance to protest, and demanded that he drive on. He didn't argue, he could see from the look in her eyes that whatever had happened to this girl, the explanations could wait until they were driving along.

Nat knew that her next destination was a place called Troywood. If she could make her way to that place, she could be reunited with her family as Doctor Pierce had already revealed.

She did not even know her current location let alone where Troywood was situated.

Using the lorry driver's sat nav and map, and taking every care not to leave a trail on security cameras, Nat gradually navigated her way along the

UK's motorways, scrounging food and drink, using truckers' facilities to stay clean and relying on the goodwill of drivers to get her there safely.

Such was the rural location of Troywood, she ended up making the final parts of the journey on foot, cutting across fields and woodland in the process.

So it was that Nat found herself finally reunited with her family in the Secret Bunker.

Concealed in her pocket was data which could be used to destroy the entire population of a planet.

Quadrant 1: Troywood, Fife (Unification: T-minus 22 minutes)

James stood in front of the control panel which he'd successfully operated not that long ago. So much seemed to have happened since he let Amy and Nat into the building – and Simon too, as he had found out later in the briefing session.

He was looking at the panel now, but he was struggling to remember what he'd done to operate the blast doors. Why couldn't he remember? He cursed the device in his neck, assuming that it was responsible in some way. The sooner they disabled these things, the better.

He and Simon were successfully reunited on the third level; they blended in with Kate's security teams and managed to avoid detection as they moved through the bunker.

The level of activity in Quadrant 1 was massive – Kate was very obviously on the verge of deploying her new army of Troopers. That probably meant that they'd be breaching the remaining Quadrants imminently. And he was sure that making their way back through Quadrant 1 would be nowhere near as easy as it had been, once those new troops were deployed.

James understood the gravity of this mission. He had to disable the mobile mast on the ground above to release Kate's team from whatever – whoever – it was that was controlling them.

At least he was free from the threat of the drones. He didn't envy the Beijing team who were having to disable multiple masts within a city that was under constant missile attack from the drones. They had to make their way through the rubble of many destroyed areas to disable all of the mobile masts that served the massive city. His was an easy mission by comparison.

He got the feeling that Simon was keeping something back from him. He kept emphasizing how important it was that James was back at the bunker doors within a twenty-minute window.

Twenty minutes to reach the surface, blow up the mast and run back again. It was a tight window – he knew that he'd struggle, particularly with the visor and breathing equipment that he had to wear to avoid being overcome by the darkness beyond the blast doors.

He struggled once again to recall what he'd done earlier. It was like trying to remember a dream. You got the overall sense of it, but it was impossible to pull out the detail.

He'd got it, by focusing on all the events before and after. That way he'd managed to close in on what he'd done to activate the panel.

'Remember James, I'm going to hide for twenty minutes after we open this door. I'll be back to let you in in twenty minutes exactly, if I can access this area again afterwards. If it's blocked, you'll have to sit this thing out on the surface with everybody else.'

James closed his eyes, and pressed the buttons using the memories that he'd dredged up from the depths of his mind.

The blast doors began to open, slowly and heavily. The protective force field activated in front of them to defend against the darkness beyond. James ran. 'Back in twenty minutes!' he shouted.

Outside the blast doors James became just a disembodied voice, Simon could see nothing. He closed the doors, noted the way that James had operated them in the first place, then prepared to make himself scarce.

The alarms were sounding, and although he was confident that he could cope with a small team of Kate's security guards, he knew that he stood no chance against the Troopers if they were deployed.

Simon looked at the countdown on his Comms-Tab, carefully synchronized with James's.

He'd taken a risk playing confidant to Doctor Pierce, particularly in the light of the sabotage that was responsible for the deadly events taking place within this Quadrant.

He hadn't revealed anything about their plans, but he'd taken Pierce at his word over Unification. He knew it would be a tight window, but James had to get that mast disabled.

If he wasn't back in twenty minutes, Simon wasn't sure that he could protect him from what was about to follow.

Chapter Six

Quadrant 3: White Sulphur Springs, West Virginia (Unification: T-minus 19 minutes)

Mike was anxious to squeeze out the last of the final seconds before Xiang's meeting. He'd barely read the text message on his Comms-Tab. He was totally engrossed in two coding projects on his screens. Magnus's guys were good, they'd share information with him as they got it, and Mike would assimilate it and build it into his own work.

They'd got lucky. One of the tech staff had found the drones folder and they'd merged it with additional data that Simon had retrieved from the Quadrant 1 Operations Centre. They'd also managed to get some basic information about the neck devices. Neuronic Devices as the documentation referred to them, shortened to 'Neuros' in many of the text files.

Magnus was right about them being linked to the mobile masts. They used another frequency which was bounced all over the planet using the existing infrastructure. Very clever. And a little last minute according to the files.

The dates indicated that this was existing technology introduced into the Genesis 2 project much later, due to deadline pressures. Hence the use of mobile masts by the look of it. He was more worried by the way that the Neuros were allocated.

Quadrant personnel were allocated red, yellow, green and purple devices. Each one operated on an individual frequency, via the mobile network. There was nothing in the files about the blue devices. The ones used on his wife and her friend James. Or

'Roachie' as she insisted on calling him.

It was the black devices which bothered him most though. They didn't use the same system as the others. The mobile masts made no difference to them, they formed their own network. So the black devices were used like bees in a hive or ants in a nest. The Troopers were using them to sustain a group consciousness. There was a Queen, and it was the Queen that had to be destroyed to break the link. But where was the Queen? Who – or what – was the Queen?

On his second screen, Mike watched the data array complete filtering and analysis after running for over thirty minutes. So many codes, so much information. He'd had to use his best tech tricks to accelerate the process.

The bunker shook as the missile from another drone exploded on the ground high above them. Alarms sounded in the corridor outside – there was momentary confusion and panic. They'd sustained structural damage. The drones were beginning to erode the defensive layers that separated them from the surface high above.

At least that's one problem that they could now solve. He finally had the codes to disable the drones.

Shamed

At first he'd been pivotal to the early successes of The Global Consortium. His brilliant mind, his scientific innovation, his ability to find creative solutions where there seemed to be so few options available. He'd been an integral part of the team, working alongside world leaders, instrumental in combining talent from around the world to make incredible strides forward. But it was a disaster waiting to happen.

The massive power and the huge budgets fanned the flames of his psychosis, and it was not long before he was unable to help himself. As well as nurturing the work of the Genesis 2 project, he started up a few side projects of his own, unwittingly funded by The Global Consortium. They ran for over two years until he was discovered. He was relieved of his duties due to 'ethical conflicts'.

He believed to his core that it was acceptable to experiment on live creatures – humans – particularly when the safety of the planet was at stake. The Global Consortium begged to differ. He was furious. He vowed revenge on the government leaders who had disowned him. How dare they question his processes? Didn't they know that he was a genius and that he alone could save the planet from these threats?

His megalomania was only fuelled by the actions of The Global Consortium and, in hindsight, they should probably have monitored him more closely after the inquiry. That event had involved two of their most senior project managers – two brilliant scientists who together had been entrusted with the future of the planet. One had been investigated after a series of simulations went badly wrong, resulting in the serious injury of two of the recruits. The other investigated for unacceptable medical and experimental behaviours which had resulted in completely unethical experimentation being carried out.

Both were brilliant men, but their motivations were different. One had made an error of judgement which was forgivable in the circumstances, though entirely unacceptable. The other had committed a crime against humanity – he was lucky that his current immunity under the Genesis 2 project spared him from prosecution and incarceration.

These two brilliant scientists came as a pair. They had studied together as young men and their brilliance had come about because of that deep bond between them. They were brothers. More than brothers. They were twins. Identical twins.

Yet one was born with a compelling desire to do harm, to wreak havoc and create destruction. The other was a good man, who tried to guide his brother, but knew that deep inside he couldn't help himself.

And so it was that Doctor Harold Pierce was permitted to stay with the Genesis 2 project, whilst his furious twin, Henry, was let go from the project.

Doctor Henry Pierce had a brilliant mind and was given unlimited access to one of the most important global projects ever carried out. But now he had become a bitter, resentful man, wildly jealous of his twin brother and part of Genesis 2 for long enough to form alliances which would ultimately place the future of the planet precariously in his hands.

Docked

High above the Earth, there was movement around one of the larger satellites which formed the main hub of the giant matrix. It was a small spaceship, not of human origin, and it approached from outside the matrix, undetected by the man who was currently consulting once again with The Global Consortium of world leaders.

This was not part of the plan that had been so

many years in the making. The ship docked noiselessly with the spherical orb, unseen and unnoticed. There was a boarding party ready. It was made up of twenty Troopers, each of them heavily armed for combat, just the same as those which had been activated in Quadrant 1. Embedded within their necks were pulsating black lights. The devices enabled them to speak directly to their Queen.

At the head of the boarding party were two people. One was a middle-aged man. He wore a lab coat on which was pinned a lapel badge. It read 'Dr H. Pierce'.

At his side was a figure which was neither man nor beast. He was not of this planet. His name was Zadra Nurmeen and he had forged an evil alliance with the man at his side.

They boarded the orb and stormed into its central Ops Area. Brother faced brother, twin was reunited with twin.

'Henry ...' said the gentler looking twin, taken aback to see his brother after so many years, yet not altogether surprised.

He had suspected this from the moment the lights failed to come on in time in Quadrant 1. There were only two other people who knew these systems as well as he did: Doctor Henry Pierce and Zadra Nurmeen, who had also been thrown off the Genesis 2 project at the same time as his brother. Who'd been spotted by the human participants in the second botched simulation, which had caused so much trouble for him as well.

In the instant that he saw them, it all made perfect sense to Harold Pierce. These two disaffected scientists had formed an alliance, intent on disrupting the Genesis 2 project. He'd known about his brother's illness. He'd tried his best to focus his brilliant mind on the positive work of The Global Consortium, but in the end Henry had engineered his own downfall.

Try as he might, he was unable to help his brother. Now Henry was here to seek his revenge. Harold Pierce knew that it would come eventually. As surely as he'd spitefully poured boiling water over his twin as a child, Henry Pierce would now torment Earth with the same degree of amorality that he had shown to his brother and family all those years ago.

Quadrant 4: Dixia Cheng, Beijing (Unification: T-minus 17 minutes)

Xiang had left her Quadrant in the capable hands of her deputy. As the drones continued to fire their missiles into the city above them, Xiang wept a silent tear for the people who were losing their lives because of their inability to stop these missile strikes. She knew that each time the bunker shook to its core, more people were losing their lives in the city above her, which was gradually being reduced to rubble each time one of the evil weapons found its target.

Several teams had been deployed to the surface to blow up the mobile masts. The drones had done some of that work for them, but in a city serving several million citizens, the mobile infrastructure was extensive.

Each team was equipped with resources that they'd located in the levels beneath the main bunker. With visors and breathing equipment to help them avoid the effects of the darkness, they moved over the rubble like a post-apocalyptic army – a hint of what was to come if they were unable to stop the current sabotage of the planet.

Xiang knew that the information she held on her E-Pad was far more important than this. It was greater than any discovery she'd made to date and its effects more far-reaching for humanity. She tried to wipe thoughts of her burning city from her mind. The teams would do their work on the surface, they would disable the masts. She must focus on the bigger picture.

Xiang had waited a short time before transportation to Quadrant 3, taking a few minutes to think things through, to pay her respects to her countrymen who were losing their lives in the city above her.

She'd seen things in the last twenty-four hours which even as a scientist she struggled to comprehend. Now she had to deliver this terrible information to the twins – and their parents.

Xiang placed her hand on the activation panel. The SymNode did its job, and transported her across the world to Quadrant 3. Ten minutes after she left her bunker, using the very same Transporter in which she'd made her exit, the first contingent of Troopers arrived from Quadrant 1.

The small security team which had been assigned to monitor the Transporter were annihilated within seconds. They were simply no match for these war machines.

With control of Quadrants 2 and 4 now secured, there was only Quadrant 3 to go and Kate's takeover would be absolute.

Chapter Seven

Quadrant 3: White Sulphur Springs, West Virginia (Unification: T-minus 12 minutes)

We're all back in a briefing room on Level 1, only this time all essential personnel are here, and James and Simon are on live feeds via their Comms-Tabs. Xiang wants to see me, Nat, Mum and Dad in a separate room before the main briefing begins. Dad is clearly excited with his own news, but Xiang makes it clear that this is about her agenda.

'I'm so sorry that I have to tell you this information like this, Amy and Mike. I know you would have wanted to do this more gently. I'm afraid that we have no time, I must share this information with you now, and it will be difficult for you to hear.'

Xiang's voice softens. 'Dan and Nat, do you know that you are adopted?'

For a moment I'm relieved. If this is all she's going to tell us it will be fine. Mum and Dad are very open about these things and we know that Mum can't have children of her own – they told us when they decided to bring David into the family. David was told that he was adopted when Harriet joined us.

'They know that already,' Mum says. 'Is that what this is about?'

Xiang puts her hand up.

'One moment,' she continues. 'Amy and Mike, did you ever meet Dan and Nat's natural parents?'

'No,' says Dad. 'All we knew is that their mother had died in childbirth and their father was unknown.'

'That makes sense,' says Xiang.

Okay, I'm beginning to learn things now. Mum

and Dad had always told us that we could meet our parents if we wanted to when we were older. They don't appear to have been telling us the whole truth.

'Please prepare for what I'm about to tell you. There is no easy way to break this news,' Xiang continues.

She looks nervous about what she is about to say: it's not the first time I've seen a face like that in the past forty-eight hours.

'Dan and Nat, your DNA is only part human … One of your parents must have been human, but your DNA strands, they are like nothing I have ever seen before.'

Nobody speaks. We just look at each other. Xiang breaks the silence.

'I'm sorry to tell you in this way, but there's more information I need to share with you.'

I'm not sure if any of us are capable of taking more information on board, but Xiang continues regardless.

'I sent my teams back to check this again, we had to be sure that it was correct. When Nat and Dan were reunited again, it triggered something between them.'

'We know,' says Nat. 'We've always known that we were hooked up in some way.'

'We've observed already how you seem to experience enhanced brain function as part of your unique biological makeup Nat, but this is more serious I'm afraid.'

Once again, I don't like the sound of this. Nat and I knew that something had happened once we were reunited, but Xiang's face is showing us all we need to know about this latest news.

'When you met again, it triggered a NanoVirus that had been implanted in Nat. The toxicity levels in Nat's samples are 90 percent higher than in yours Dan. It seems that you coming together has triggered a viral process that has been implanted in Nat.

'It has spread from Nat to you Dan, and it will reach a critical mass across your two bodies. When it hits that critical point, your bodies will cease to function, your lives will be unsustainable.

'I estimate that you have approximately three hours until that happens.'

There is no silence this time. Nat is furious. I think she's ahead of us, but she just made a connection that the rest of us have been unable to make.

'It's Pierce again!' she says. 'I told you he was evil. This is what those experiments were for, I'll bet!

'If it's the last thing I do, I'm going to take that man down.'

Quadrant 1: Troywood, Fife (Unification: T-minus 9 minutes)

Simon now knew that there was no chance James was getting back into the bunker. From the minute the alarms sounded, the Troopers were swarming around the bunker's blast doors. He'd have to wait it out on the surface above – Plan B. If the operation was a success, and all was restored to normality in this Quadrant, he would soon be back inside.

But Simon was troubled by these Troopers and the black, pulsating lights in their necks. He hoped that blowing up the mast would disable these devices as well. He knew that James wasn't getting back in time, within that twenty-minute window. He hoped that he'd be okay out there. But this had to be done.

'Ready to detonate!' announced James over the Comms-Tab.

'Make sure you're clear,' Simon replied. 'Then get out of there, take cover away from the bunker.'

'Why not in the cottage?' asked James, thrown by the change of plan.

'Just blow the mast then get away from the cottage!' Simon shouted.

Simon heard the blast over the Comms-Tab. He heard James running. He hoped that he'd get away in time because Simon knew that there were four Troopers out there now hunting him down. They'd left the bunker shortly after the alarm had been sounded.

James was on his own.

Quadrant 3: White Sulphur Springs, West Virginia (Unification: T-minus 7 minutes)

After Xiang's last announcement, none of us knows what to say, so when Magnus ushers us all into the larger meeting room, it's actually a welcome relief. We need a few minutes to make sense of this latest information.

Dad is desperate to report his news. 'We can stop the drones,' he says. 'We have the codes.' The bunker shakes once again as a missile strikes the surface high above us. This time the lights flicker momentarily, but they don't fail.

Magnus brings up a screen on the main monitor, Dad sends the codes to his E-Pad, and we all watch the drones on a world map, each one steadily heading towards its target. There are still many of them in the air. Magnus enters the codes, his fingers adept at using digital keypads at speed. It happens in an instant. One second each drone icon has a red light in the middle of it, then the next they're gone. There is a round of applause, and for a split second me, Mum, Nat and Dad forget the news that we've just received from Xiang.

'Congratulations Mike,' says Magnus. 'Excellent work!'

Next we patch into James's Comms-Tab. He'll be the first to bring down the most important mast above Quadrant 1. We listen in to an exchange between him and Simon. We hear the explosion as he runs off away from the mast. We're about to applaud once again, expecting any moment now that the mast will fall and disable the devices which are currently controlling Kate and her team in Quadrant 1. But instead we hear shots being fired over the Comms-Tab feed. At first it's not clear who's shooting. But there is more than one weapon being fired here, and James is running fast – we can hear his breathing. He's running for his life. There's another shot fired. Then there is a thud on the ground and James's breathing stops.

Unification: T-minus zero minutes

The Karman line is the place where the Earth's atmosphere and the beginning of space meet. In a spherical space station orbiting in space, a middle-aged man is struck in anger by his twin brother as he pushes him away from the control desk where he has been orchestrating events on the planet below.

Almost two hundred shocked faces watch these

events. These are the faces of the world's leaders. They cannot intervene because their bodies are currently in stasis on the planet below. But they are conscious of everything that is happening here and they are acutely aware of its gravity, but they are just hologram images and are helpless in this scenario.

These leaders once banished this man from the project which he now controls. He is accompanied by another who they offended, this one even more unpredictable, because he is of a species which does not live on Earth. Under the control of this vitriolic partnership, the Shards which are pulsating away in the Earth, the sea, and the air, have begun to inject their poison into the planet below. They were there to heal, now they will change the planet beyond recognition, to a place that cannot be inhabited by the life forms which have existed there for millions of years.

The Earth has begun to burn.

In the skies, clusters of drones head towards their final destination. They are unarmed now. They will simply drop out of the clouds as they run out of fuel, neutered of the power they once wielded. But hidden deep beneath the Black Sea, known only to one man, are fifty nuclear submarines, already activated and simply awaiting a set of coordinates.

There are four Quadrants positioned around the globe. Their inhabitants were supposed to be the Custodians of the terraforming process, watching on as the world healed. A powerful army of cybernetically enhanced Troopers now has full control over three of the Quadrants. They have just begun to prepare for transportation to the fourth and final Quadrant.

A short distance away from the burning phone mast at Troywood, a man lies in the grass. The mast is destroyed, but he has been shot whilst trying to secure this small victory.

Within the heart of Quadrant 3, a viral time bomb is ticking deep inside the bodies of the twins in whose hands the safety of the planet resides. They are pivotal in this mission, but they have only hours left before their lives are terminated, taken away by an evil, vindictive scientist.

A countdown process reaches its end on the doctor's console in space, seen too late by his twin brother who is shouting instructions to his army of Troopers. There is a deep and steady rumble within the lower two levels of each of the four Quadrants. This is not an attack from the drones. They have been stopped. Something unexpected is happening beneath the bunkers. There is a massive surge of power and they begin to move from their location deep within the ground. The lower Quadrant sections start to separate from the levels above them and begin to rise.

One at a time, the lower two levels of each bunker erupt through the ground which contains them, casting aside rocks, trees and grass as they do so. The upper two levels of the bunkers remain completely intact, each one was built to accommodate these sleeping giants in a vast underground frame. This is Unification.

It was never supposed to happen, but The Global Consortium has ordered this. As the Earth begins to die below the four hovering Quadrants, they move towards a central destination high above Europe. There they will merge to create a massive, circular ship. This ship will become an ark for humanity, but also the source of its protection. It will join with a spherical space station currently forming the hub of a vast matrix above the Earth and known as The Nexus. It is here that Earth's final battle will be fought, in space, hundreds of kilometres above the surface of the planet.

As the lower levels of Quadrant 1 start to rise above the bunker in Scotland, a woman by the name of Kate briefly touches her neck. The red light which pulsed there only minutes ago has now stopped. She feels strangely different and she's not entirely sure what's going on. She knows it's not good, she can feel the tense atmosphere among the Control Room staff, but as she focuses on the half-human, half-robot figures around her, she's very sure of one thing.

Whatever is going on here, she's going to fix it.

The Secret Bunker Trilogy concludes in Part 3: Regeneration ...

Deal

The deal was done – it was sealed by a handshake. They had been disowned by the leaders who once celebrated their wisdom. Both harboured hateful grudges against the very people who had previously been their friends and colleagues. Deep inside, they incubated a contempt of humanity, an unstoppable urge to destroy and dominate.

There were many buyers interested in the planet known as 'Earth'. As it was, inhabited by a vast array of different species, it was untouchable under interplanetary laws. But if the terraforming went wrong, if the planet were to die?

Well, that would be another story.

The Queen

The Troopers worked as one, controlled by The Queen. She was all powerful, they never even thought to question her commands. They would receive their instructions via the black devices buried within their necks.

They had been culled from humanity, the finest physical specimens enhanced by incredible technology. All answerable to their Queen, who was part of this Unholy Trinity. But nobody knew who she was.

She was able to control this dangerous army with complete anonymity. And so it would remain until the final battle.

Launch

He took a deep breath as he carefully keyed in the coordinates sketched out on his console. He had been here before. Where life and death were precariously balanced on a knife edge and brave decisions and terrible risks had to be taken to preserve lives.

But who knew how things would play out if these missiles reached their targets?

He confirmed the coordinates and it was done.

Deep beneath the Black Sea, fifty submarine drones were armed in an instant. Each one carried a massive nuclear payload. Within the hour, they would reach their final destination.

Birth

The twins were beautiful. They looked exactly like the doctor said they would. The human genes were dominant – they would blend in perfectly on this planet. They would remain undetected, able to live a normal life.

Each one was perfectly formed, a boy and a girl. But she would be compelled to abandon her children on Earth and trust the humans to show them the kindness that they had offered to herself and her husband.

She had to return to her own planet to face trial by the Elders. She had committed the ultimate crime. She had revealed to the humans that there was life elsewhere among the stars.

More details via The Secret Bunker Trilogy website at http://thesecretbunker.net

PLEASE LEAVE A REVIEW

If you enjoyed The Secret Bunker: The Four Quadrants please leave a review on Amazon to help more readers to discover the trilogy – thank you!

http://thesecretbunker.net/review2

ABOUT THE AUTHOR

Paul Teague has worked as a waiter, a shopkeeper, a primary school teacher, a disc jockey and a radio journalist and broadcaster for the BBC. He wrote his first book at the age of 9 years old. The hand-written story received the inevitable rejection slip, but that didn't stop him dabbling with writing throughout his life. The Secret Bunker Trilogy was inspired by a family visit to 'Scotland's Secret Bunker' at Troywood in Fife, Scotland.

Printed in Great Britain
by Amazon